TOO LATE FOR SHADOWS AND MEMORIES

Madison,
Watch out for backflips!
Piper Badwell
♡ you Glitter Bitch!

AND MEMORIES

Too Late for Shadows and Memories

PIPER BEDWELL

Piper Bedwell

Copyright © 2022 by Piper Bedwell

All rights reserved. No part of this book may be reproduced in any manner whatsoever without written permission except in the case of brief quotations embodied in critical articles and reviews.

First Printing, 2022

Second verse, same as the first. No really...
Thank you to my friends and family for putting up with my craziness of publishing two books in the same year, much less 3 months apart. Huge thanks to Jarrad and Beccah for going through this process again in such a short amount of time. And to my girls, Tali and Lina, you are my world!

Chapter 1

Bag slung over her shoulder, she ran down the carpeted stairs and into the living room. Her entire body was on alert as she crossed into the kitchen. Flinging open one of the drawers, she rummaged through the junk inside until her fingers felt the cool steel of the one thing she was looking for.

Realistically, Fiona knew a knife was no match for a bullet, but it was all she had. She hurried back to the living room in search for her keys. Finding her flip flops along the way, she wracked her brain trying to remember where she had put them. She mentality retraced her steps from the moment she had arrived five point two five minutes ago.

She face palmed herself as she realized her mistake. They were still in the car, which was still running. Her speedy get away awaited just outside. She sprinted to the front door, her flip flops click clacking on her feet, and flung open the door.

Ice water ran through her veins as her eyes fell on the suit clad man before her. Her mind simultaneously raced and emptied of all thought as his lips curled into a menacing smile. She staggered backwards, trying to put space between the two of them as her eyes darted around, looking for any way out.

"You should have called," his icy voice cooed as he stalked towards her. "You know I hate unscheduled visits at the office."

***

Air rushed into her lungs as Mackenzie bolted upright. Her eyes darted around the room, ensuring she was alone in her bedroom. Her hands gripped the comforter tightly, trying desperately to ground herself in reality and push all memories of her past away. Seeing that nothing was amiss, she forced her breathing to slow as she scrubbed her hands over her face.

"Just another damn dream," she mumbled to herself as she flopped back onto the bed.

Her head rolled to one side and stared at the clock beside her pillow. 7:00 am. She had shut her eyes only four short hours prior. Instead of cursing her short-lived slumber, she was glad she had gotten as much as she had. Sleep was no longer a close friend of hers.

Rolling out of bed, she stumbled to the bathroom, resigned to get ready for the day. After a quick shower, she dressed in her athletic capris and a tight-fitting tank top and headed for the living room after ensuring her chestnut hair was securely in a messy bun. Blue eyes stared back at her in a wall mounted mirror as she passed. A stranger that just happened to have her freckles was who met her every day. This was her new reality.

After sliding on her shoes, she grabbed her cell phone and keys and threw them into her gym bag as she headed for the front door. She paused long enough to put on her sunglasses, which were on the table by the entrance, before stepping outside.

The warmth of the day greeted her like an old friend. It was another day in paradise, or as close to paradise as she was ever going to find. The sky was clear, the sun shined brightly, and a light ocean breeze drifted by. The wide streets were crowded with cars as people made their way to work, making her thankful that she didn't own a vehicle.

She hadn't gone far before she reached her destination. The gym wasn't overly fancy, but it had everything she needed and not so overcrowded that she had an audience. She had never really been a pumping iron kind of woman, but a few rounds in the ring, kick boxing against the biggest guy she could find was what she considered fun these days.

As she stepped inside and removed her sunglasses, she looked around. Empty. No one to stare at her, yet, no one to spar with either. Deciding it was probably for the best, she made her way to the punching bags in the far back corner and sat her bag down. Sliding her shoes off, she began the tedious yet comforting task of carefully wrapping her hands and feet before reaching for her earbuds and gloves.

The heavy bass from her music radiated through her body as she stretched out her overly tight muscles. Bouncing from foot to foot, she rolled her shoulders and neck, getting into the beat from her headphones. A few practice jabs, a kick or two, and she was ready to go, ready to drown out the nightmares that plagued her.

Two hours and several songs later, her arms and legs felt like lead, but her mind was blissfully quiet. She sat on the bench with a towel to her face as the few people that had finally shown up milled around the room. While some of her normal sparing partners had eventually arrived, they knew when to give her a wide path and when it was safe to interact.

After freshening up as best she could, she stepped back out into the bustling city around her. A smile sprang to her face as her phone rang. She quickly changed her headphones out for her blue tooth head set and answered the call.

"Jade!" she greeted, crossing the street and dodging pedestrians.

"Mac! What's up, girl?" Jade exclaimed, excitement dripping from her voice.

"Leaving the gym, you?" Mackenzie offered casually. "And why are you awake? Isn't it like four AM?"

"Yeah, something like that. I couldn't sleep, have to get up soon anyway so I thought I'd check in," Jade explained.

"When did you stop sleeping?" Mackenzie asked. "You know what, don't answer that. I'm pretty sure I know."

The two sat in a chilled silence for a few moments. Mackenzie entered the heart of the city, a pedestrian zone, while Jade, from the sounds of containers opening and closing, put on her makeup for the day.

"It's supposed to be warm today in Atlanta. What about you? Any plans?" Jade questioned, lightening the mood.

"It's already hot here," Mackenzie confirmed, looking at the active volcano in the distance. "But I don't work tonight so I'll probably just grab food and watch a movie."

"What? No hot date? Come on!" Jade teased. She had been pushing her best friend for years to 'get back on the horse.'

"Jade..." Mackenzie warned.

"What?! I'm not saying to fall in love with the guy, but a little lust wouldn't hurt things. A girl has needs!"

"Whoa whoa whoa..." Mackenzie began before being cut off once more.

"Find a hot body and go for it! I mean, damn, you like food! Let someone else pay for it and then have an ACTUAL conversation with someone of the opposite sex who's nice to look at."

"Right, food and conversation. That's what we're talking about here," Mackenzie commented sarcastically.

"I mean...wherever the night goes from there is up to you," Jade replied casually. Mackenzie could just see her best friend looking innocently at her nails in mock interest.

"Sure sure. Not gonna happen. I'm just fine on my own," Mackenzie confirmed as she made her way through the growing crowd of people.

"I'm an old married woman, now. I live vicariously through you and you aren't doing either of us any favors. I'm just saying..."

"Yeah, well, you need to find someone else to live through, it seems. I totally make the best life choices," Mackenzie laughed.

La Pescheria was in full swing that morning and the noise level proved it. The daily fish market was the oldest in the city and was sure to pull people in from all around for freshly caught sea food. Other than catching it yourself, this was the freshest you could find. Sometimes, it was even still breathing.

"What is that sound?" Jade asked above the deafening levels.

"A local market. I'll get through here as quickly as I can," Mackenzie promised.

"Is that Italian I hear?" Jade asked above the deafening levels.

"Nope, Spanish," Mackenzie lied. Her best friend was always trying to guess where Mackenzie was living, but it was too dangerous to tell her. This time, she was too close.

"Then why don't I understand it? I speak Spanish," Jade reminded her.

"Because they are yelling and all talking at once. Also, dialect. Can we just drop it? You know why I can't tell you where I am," Mackenzie reminded her, making her way towards a quieter part of town.

"Fine, but if you stop calling one day, how am I supposed to know where to look?" Jade asked, a slight tremble in her voice.

"You're not."

Mackenzie hated shutting her down, but she couldn't risk her knowing anything that could get either of them killed. She continued walking for a few moments as the silence stretched over the line.

"Jade," she began regretfully.

"No, I know, and you're right," Jade said reluctantly. Forcing cheer back into her voice, she continued. "So where are you going right now?"

"There is this cute little café that I've found. I need coffee," Mackenzie answered, relieved at the change in topic.

The rest of the conversation was lighthearted enough. Jade told her of her upcoming projects at work and Mackenzie danced around anything that would give away her current city of choice. The separation was always hard, but at least they could talk occasionally.

Mackenzie stepped into the quaint little café and almost immediately silenced her phone. Coming to her own conclusions was different than Jade hearing Mackenzie order her coffee in Italian. She unmuted the line as she made her way to a quiet table towards the back.

"Did I lose you? The line went really quiet..." Jade commented, trying to get her attention.

Before Mackenzie could respond once more, a tall shadow drifted into her path seconds before the solid body that accompanied it followed. Mackenzie was usually pretty quick on her feet, but her momentum and one-track mind worked against her. Trying desperately to stop in time, she, instead, ran face first into the immovable object, hot coffee raining down on her.

"Shit! That's hot! Dammit! Sorry!" she rambled, trying to right herself and pull her body off of the one in her path.

"Mac! Are you okay?" Jade yelled in her ear.

"Are you okay? Let me help you," a deep male voice offered. The sound washed over her, melting her insides and sending a tingling down her spine.

"Did you run into someone?" Jade laughed.

"It's okay...I've got it," Mackenzie assured the man before her, pulled from her stupor by Jade's laughter. "Wait, you're American?"

Almost everyone in this tourist town spoke English on some level, but it was rare to find an American in this part of the city. Her eyes finally lifted from her coffee-soaked shirt. Emerald green eyes stared back at her with a smile that extended from his perfectly shaped mouth.

"You did! You totally ran into someone. He sounds hot! Is he?! Oh, please, tell me he's hot!" Jade prattled on excitedly.

"I am," he chuckled, answering more questions than he knew were asked. "As are you, apparently. Is that a problem?"

"No, of course not! It's just..." Mackenzie paused and looked around quickly.

"Don't worry, tourists aren't taking over your favorite hide out," he assured her, understanding her unspoken fear.

"I'm assuming from your lack of answer that he's hot!" Jade commented.

"How do you know I'm not a tourist just trying to get away from the rest of them?" Mackenzie asked, trying to slow her racing heart.

"Can you ask him to speak up? I'm really having to strain here," Jade continued.

"The way you ordered your coffee. The accent and the confidence that screams 'I live here'," he told her.

"You were watching me order?" Mackenzie questioned, suddenly unsure of his motives.

"A woman as beautiful as you is bound to be noticed in anything she does," he admitted, his eyes sparkling with mischief.

"Oh my god! He's hot AND charming!" Jade squealed. "And he's freaking flirting with you!"

"I...I don't know about that," Makenzie stammered, a blush rising on her cheeks at his compliment. "I just left the gym so I'm sweaty and now covered in coffee..."

"Shut up and take the damn compliment!" Jade chastised in her ear. "Don't scare him off! Dinner! Remember?! Conversation?!"

"The coffee part is my fault," he stated sheepishly. "Let me make it up to you. Dinner. Tonight. My treat. And you can try to convince me that you could ever be more beautiful than you are right now."

"You better say 'yes' Mac!" Jade yelled.

"I...um..." Mackenzie's mind reeled, making thought impossible.

"Unless you already have plans," he commented, giving her a way out.

"Nope! She's going out with you instead of being a lonely bum at home alone!" Jade answered for her, knowing he couldn't hear her.

"I mean...I don't even..."

"Of course, how rude of me. I'm Nicolai, but you can call me Niko," he introduced.

"I'm Mackenzie," she replied, starting to feel a little more at ease.

"But you can call her anything you want, hot stuff!"

"Good-bye, Jade," Mackenzie whispered as she disconnected her phone, Jade yelling her protest till the end.

"I'm sorry?" Nicolai asked quizzically.

"Sorry, I was just-"

"Mac!" the barista called out, cutting her explanation off.

Mackenzie whipped around as the woman came towards her with her coffee.

"Mac, huh? I would've assumed you'd go by Kenzie, but somehow, Mac seems to fit you better," Nicolai teased as she took her offered coffee.

As she turned back to him, her eyes slowly raked over his body. His voice was just the first dreamy thing about him. Even through his t-shirt, she could tell he was built. His solid chest paired nicely with his wide shoulders. The slow smile that crept along his perfectly chiseled, neatly bearded jaw told her without words that she had been caught staring.

"I'm sorry, what were you saying?" she asked, embarrassed that her brain had abandoned her.

"You were saying that you would go out with me tonight," he answered smugly.

"I don't usually-"

"-give a guy a snowballs chance in Hell?" he interrupted her as she tried to step around him to get to her table.

"Well, I mean...I wouldn't...I..." Makenzie took a deep breath and tried to calm her nerves. She tried to think of all the reasons she should say 'no', but her friend's advice rang louder than the rest. It's not like he was asking her to marry him. It was one night. Dinner and conversation. What could go wrong? The answer tumbled out of her mouth before she could stop it. "Sure."

"Perfect! I'll pick you up at six." His smile lit his face and put one on hers as well.

She quickly wrote down her address and phone number on a napkin before she lost her nerve and changed her mind.

"See you at six," she whispered as he walked away, his cologne lingering even after he had gone.

She made her way to her preferred table and sat down. What had just happened? What had she just agreed to? Men had asked her out over the years, but she had easily told them 'no'. Nicolai was the first in years to make her want to say 'yes' and the only one she had actually done so. Was it just her best friends voice that had her changing her tune, or was it his intensely green eyes and playful smirk?

Sitting down, she took a sip of her coffee and closed her eyes. The taste soothed her nerves and her mind slowly began to clear. "Oh shit," she muttered, her eyes flying open. "I have to go shopping!"

***

Mackenzie stared at herself in the bathroom mirror, checking over her handy work. Brown hair hung in soft waves around her shoulders and blue eyes stared back at her. She exhaled slowly.

"I'll never get used to this," she said out loud in the empty apartment.

She scrubbed her hands over her face before reaching for her makeup bag. She began applying eye shadow as she thought about the night to come. She was still shocked at her answer when he asked her out, but what shocked her more was that he had asked. She had looked like a literal hot mess while he had looked like he had just stepped out of a GQ magazine.

She remembered the slow smile that crossed his face and the mischievous glint in his eyes as he looked at her. Even the thought of it was enough to make her heart race and her breathing halt. No one had looked at her like that in ...well...a very long time. It reminded her of a time when anything was possible, and her entire life was before her.

"That's why I agreed to this," she tried to convince herself, "and not the butterflies in my stomach just the sound of his voice sent into flight."

No matter how well tonight went, that was as far as things could go. She didn't have the luxury of butterflies and all they implied. Butterflies meant attraction, attraction led to romance, and romance led to heartbreak when she left. And she *would* leave. Not only could she not do that to herself, she couldn't do that to another living soul. Especially not when she couldn't explain why.

"It's just one night, and it's just dinner," she reminded herself, inspecting her face.

She was accustomed to doing her makeup daily for work, but this was the first time she had done makeup for a first date in over a decade. It was nerve wracking to say the least. Deciding it was perfect, she left the bathroom and stood outside her closet door. Hanging before her, was every normal woman's go-to date outfit, a little black dress.

Jade had been overjoyed when Mackenzie had finally answered her return call that morning and even more excited that Mackenzie had agreed to the date. Thankful for her best friend's fashion advice, Mackenzie had all but begged her for help on what to wear. They had talked through the finer points of clothing, strapless, halter, off the shoulder, V-neck, scoop neck, sweetheart, and decided that sticking as close to classic lines as possible was her best bet. While she wanted to look nice, she wanted to feel comfortable in her own skin as well.

With that in mind, the dress she found was a sleeveless, V-neck bandage style, that was tight fitting and showed off her more than ample chest and curves. Her dress code at work was already tight fitting, so that was pretty normal for her now, but she had conceded to her besties expertise on flaunting her larger than usual chest. While she had shown it off once upon a time, now it just caused unwanted attention.

"Tonight is about attention," she reminded herself, her besties words ringing in her ears as her hands ran over the fabric before her.

With one last resigned sigh, she pulled her confidence out of the gutter and grabbed the dress off the hanger. She slid into the garment, thankful for her flexibility as she zipped herself in. She dug her trusty stilettos out of her closet and searched for a clutch. Thankfully, due to her current job, clutches were a must and her shoes were fully broken in. No sore feet on a date for this girl.

Her phone chimed, pulling her away from her search for the perfect handbag for her outfit. Looking down, she didn't recognize the number, but the message told her the sender could only be one person.

"Niko."

'See you in 5' was all the message read. Simple. Straightforward. Not at all flirty. So why did it send tingles along her spine?

Looking at the time, she realized he was going to be right on time. She quickly decided on a rhinestone studded clutch and tossed in her essentials before sliding into her heels. She rushed back to the bathroom and searched through the cosmetics on the counter. It didn't take her long to find what she was looking for.

Leaning into the mirror, she applied the obnoxiously glittery lip gloss. Straightening back up, she looked into the full-length mirror. The body was hers, down to the curves and freckles made bolder by the Italian sun, but that's where her own recognition ended. The changes over the years had mostly been good to her, her muscles more defined, more lethal, but memories of green eyes and red hair threatened to consume her.

Pushing those memories aside, she turned off the light and continued on to her bedroom. She put the lip gloss in the clutch and made her way to the front door. She didn't want to seem overzealous for their date, but she also didn't need him in her apartment. Dinner and conversation were one thing, entering her safe space before getting to know him was something entirely different.

She looked around her humble living quarters as she waited. It was clean and tidy enough and devoid of any real personal touches. There was nothing to betray her past on the surface, but there could always be something. It was best to just meet him outside and that's what she planned to do. Then a knock sounded at the door.

She took a deep breath as she glanced at the time. 5:59. He was a minute early. Damn. Releasing her breath, she tried to calm her nerves as she plastered her brightest smile on her face.

She opened the door and her mouth went dry. If he had been handsome earlier in the coffee shop, he was nearing godlike status now. His black button down had thin purple stripes which accentuated his muscled torso. The sleeves were rolled up to his elbows, exposing his toned forearms dark wash jeans clung to his thick thighs and she found herself wondering when she could sneak a peek at his presumably perfect ass.

His deep voice pulled her from her exploration. "Hey there, beautiful."

Chapter 2

Nicolai stared at the woman before him. Somehow, even though he would never have thought it possible, she had been right. She was even more beautiful now than when they met that morning. Her long hair cascaded around her and landed on either side of her exquisite breasts. The dress she wore clung to her chest and hips, creating that hourglass look that always drove him crazy. All she needed was red hair and she would make one hell of a Jessica rabbit.

"Hey there, yourself," she replied, her own southern American accent matching his.

His eyes met hers and he could feel the air around them buzz with electricity as sparks flew between them. Nerves hit him in his gut, confusing him. This was just supposed to be another date in a long list of them. Always look unavailable by having someone on his arm, but never stay long enough that either of them got attached. That was his M.O. So, why did this one suddenly feel so different?

The sass in her eyes and the confidence in her shoulders would have been enough to fool most people, but he wasn't most people. The slight shake in her hands told him she was a bundle of nerves as well. Somehow, that both calmed him and made him more nervous.

"Ready to go?" he asked with a smile. He reached for her casually but wasn't expecting the reaction he received. Her entire body flinched involuntarily, and she took a step back. Her smile faltered but was replaced almost immediately. He held his hands out, palms forward in surrender. "I'm sorry, I was just going to offer you my arm. My momma raised a gentleman, or at least tried to."

"No, I'm sorry. I'm just a little...nervous," Mackenzie stated, kicking herself mentally for old habits.

Forcing her anxiety aside, she closed her perpetually locked door behind her and reached for his arm. She raised an eyebrow at him, questioning if his offer still stood. The smile that sprang to his face was dazzling and enough to make her knees go weak. As they walked along the sidewalk, arm in arm, she found her pulse racing with something other than anxiety.

Her eyes slid up to his face as they neared a red sportscar. His beard was short and well-trimmed, tapering to a point at his chin, elongating his face slightly and showcasing his strong jawline. His eyes lacked the creases generally called laugh lines, meaning that no matter how smooth his smile was, it rarely reached those emerald beauties. From his stance and easy demeanor, she knew he was used to having company of the opposite sex, but it would seem that they rarely pulled a true smile from him. It appeared they both had their fair share of secrets.

He opened the door to the race red auto and helped her inside. Closing the door, he circled the car and slid into the driver's seat before revving the engine and pulling into traffic. Mackenzie was a nervous wreck as they maneuvered through the city streets. She wasn't usually one to be alone with anyone anymore, much less with them driving. She looked around for the door handle in case she needed to make a quick escape at any point.

His hand caught her off guard as it softly gripped hers. Her eyes shot to his face in confusion. The sympathetic look in his eyes soothed her and released the breath she didn't know she had been holding. She forced herself to relax into the soft leather seats.

"Been a while since you went out." It was more of a statement than a question, but his eyes held no judgment.

"You could say that," she laughed, looking out the window.

"Well, don't worry. I don't bite..." His voice took on a mischievous tone. "Unless you ask. But seriously, it's just dinner. If at any point you're uncomfortable, I can either drive you home or call you a cab. Your choice."

He squeezed her hand and Mackenzie was surprised to know she was still holding his. She turned back to him, her eyes sliding from their entwined hands to his face as he watched the road.

"Thank you," she told him truthfully. "but I think I'll be just fine." She surprised herself, not because she had said that out loud, but because she meant it. Something about his touch was calming, not at all menacing or imposing. She decided to file that away to examine later.

"So, where are you taking me?" she asked, curiosity getting the best of her.

"Just a little place I've found that's out of the way. The outside leaves a lot to be desired, but once we get inside, I'm sure you'll enjoy it. I thought I would take you somewhere you've never been before," he told her, not fully answering the question.

"How do you know I've never been?" Mackenzie questioned. His raised eyebrow and sideways glance told her he had her figured out. "Right, already established I don't do this much."

"Ever," he corrected, a soft chuckle earning an annoyed glare for his efforts. "Oh, don't get your nose in a bunch. I'm not holding it against you."

"And here I thought your momma raised a gentleman," she teased.

"Tried. I said she tried. I never said she succeeded," he laughed.

"So, really, where are we going?" she pressed again.

"We're almost there, don't worry," he replied, his smile widening in anticipation.

Mackenzie narrowed her eyes at him, trying to read him but gave up before long. She didn't know him well enough to figure him out yet. She found herself pushing down the disappointment that thought brought with it. No matter how well this date went, she would never be around long enough to truly get to know the handsome man beside her.

Nicolai noticed the flash of something unspoken cross through Mackenzie's eyes. It was gone as quickly as it showed up. So quickly, that he would have missed it if not paying close attention. Things were starting to add up in his mind, a picture of the woman beside him, but he pushed them away. He could psychoanalyze her later. Tonight was about being in the moment.

He found a parking place on the street and carefully settled the expensive car into place. He flashed a grin at Mackenzie before releasing her hand and racing around to help her out.

"Afraid I would disappear if you took too long?" she jested at his quick appearance.

"Maybe I am," he replied, closing the door behind her.

He stifled a laugh at her baffled expression as she stood on the sidewalk trying to figure out where they were. He was sure she wouldn't appreciate the humor, though. She looked nervous enough to bolt at any moment. Mackenzie looked up and down the strip. Her eyes met Nicolai's and mischief flashed at her.

"You don't do well with surprises, do you?" he guessed, offering his arm to her once more.

"Not anymore," she admitted. She saw his puzzled look out of the corner of her eye, but she ignored it. That was a topic for...well...never.

"Too bad," he smirked, leading her to a non-descript building.

"Um...hold up," she stated firmly. "Why are we going to a youth hostel?" She rooted herself to the spot, refusing to move forward.

Nicolai thought about joking with her, but with the caged look in her eyes, he decided against it. "Trust me?" he asked instead, taking in her rigid stance.

"Not at all," she responded truthfully. Her eyes flew to his as soon as the words left her mouth. She searched his face for any sign that she had offended him.

His answering laugh caught her off guard and brought a smile to her own face. She found herself relaxing into him once more.

"Your honesty is refreshing," he told her as his laughter subsided. "But don't worry, no trust is required. There is a restaurant inside that's pretty unique."

"Oh...okay then," she replied, suddenly embarrassed at her reaction. "I didn't mean to imply..."

"Not at all. I can see how that would be an easy assumption," he assured her.

Together, they walked through the building and down a set of stone stairs. Soft lighting met them as the sounds of other patrons greeted them. The hostess fawned over Nicolai as Mackenzie looked around in awe.

The room was incredible. It seemed as if it had been carved directly out of the stone and dirt that normally would have occupied that space. Candles and gas lanterns lit the cave-like structure, giving everything a calm and romantic glow. The most surprising feature, however, was the river that lazily coursed through the center.

"An underground river," she mumbled to herself, trying to process it.

A satisfied smile flashed at her as Nicolai guided her to their table. His hand rested gently on the small of her back, both exciting her and easing her anxiety. She looked more closely around the room, searching for exits or hiding areas.

Nicolai thanked the overzealous hostess as he sat across from Mackenzie. He never took his eyes off of his date, making sure to establish where his attention was focused for the evening. Taking the hint, the other woman eventually left. He studied the beauty across from him as she tried to look anywhere but at him.

"Can I order us a bottle of wine?" he asked, trying to help steady her nerves.

"No, thank you. I don't usually drink," Mackenzie replied apologetically, her eyes finally meeting his. In truth, wine sounded amazing, but she couldn't take the chance.

"I don't know who in your past has made you so afraid of men, but I promise I am not that person," he told her knowingly. She had all the signs, he just wasn't sure if it had been mental or physical.

"I don't..." she stopped in the middle of her protest. Of course, he would think she was abused. She was acting like a maniac. "You know what, wine sounds great. Moscato, if you don't mind."

Nicolai motioned for the waiter and immediately ordered a bottle of their best Moscato and a hearty appetizer for them to share. He figured she would appreciate the food to soak up the alcohol as they talked, and it gave her more time to look over the menu. As the waiter left, he leaned back in his chair in a move that, he hoped, was non-threatening.

Mackenzie squirmed under his scrutiny as she tried to focus on the menu in her hands. His steady gaze pierced her like he was trying to figure out all her secrets. While she doubted he would ever fully discover what was hidden beneath, he had already gotten too close for comfort with the idea of abuse. She searched for a safe topic for conversation, anything to break the awkward silence. She settled on the elephant in the room.

"So...an underground river? Who would have thought?" She looked up at him finally and lost her breath. His eyes twinkled in the candlelight and the ambiance accentuated his devilishly handsome features.

"It runs through the entire city, but this is the best location to see it," he informed her, pulling her from her stupor. "I thought, with the smaller crowd and rhythmic sound of the water, it would be...calming."

"Okay, okay, I get it," Mackenzie smiled in spite of herself. "I'm skittish."

"Really? I hadn't noticed," he replied nobly.

"I just don't...it's been a while," she admitted. "But that is neither here nor there. We are in a beautiful setting and I am getting out of my head."

"Don't worry. Just be yourself," he encouraged.

"If only," she scoffed under her breath. "So, what's good to eat here?"

"Everything," he commented before leaning towards her. He slowly pulled the menu from her hands and laid it on the table. "Do you trust me?"

"I think we've already established this," Mackenzie laughed, this time much more relaxed than when the question was asked earlier.

A wickedly sexy grin appeared on his face and Mackenzie found herself feeling sassier than she had felt in a long time. Maybe Jade was right. A little fun once in a while wasn't a bad thing.

"Well, in this case, do you trust me enough to choose something I think you would enjoy?" he clarified, a playful glint in his eyes.

"I don't usually let-"

"-someone else be in control?" he finished, cutting her off with a chuckle.

"I was going to say, 'let others choose my food', but sure...we'll go with that," she replied, unable to hide the smile that was determined to stay on her face.

"Come on, Mac, live a little. Give up the reigns," he prodded, leaning closer.

"Give up the reins?" she repeated softly. Something familiar nagged at her.

"I just mean that I'm not asking for a commitment. If you don't like it, you can order something else," he explained, misunderstanding her comment.

"I didn't think you were, I just haven't heard that phrase in a very long time. It took me by surprise," she admitted.

"I'm sure you'll see that I'm full of surprises," he teased.

"Yeah, I am sure you are," she stated, mentally fanning herself. She had to get it together, and quick, or his charm was seriously going to work on her. Or maybe it was the easy banter between them that was doing it for her. "You know what, sure. Go right ahead, do your best."

Nicolai loved the challenge in her eyes as she stared back at him. He was so used to dating women with a pretty face, but not much going on inside the hamster wheel. It made them easier to walk away from. This woman was nothing like that. She was strong, independent, and unafraid of speaking her mind. He was sure she had frightened off her fair share of undeserving men, but it had the opposite effect on him. He found himself wondering what she would say next.

"I'm thinking the squid with plum wine sauce and those little probes to make it wiggle on your plate," he said thoughtfully.

"And you're done, off the hook for finding me food. Anything that looks at me or wiggles on my plate is..." she stopped short noticing the laughter in his eyes. "That's not even an option...is it?"

He shook his head playfully. His hair shifted with the motion and few rebellious strands tumbled over his forehead. Mackenzie suddenly found herself reaching out to brush them back in place, but caught herself before she reached them. She dropped her hand to her napkin, hoping he wouldn't notice her real intention. She pushed the thought away and narrowed her eyes at him, trying to hide her embarrassment.

"Rude," she commented, not really knowing how else to respond to his joke.

Nicolai couldn't hold in his laughter any longer. To his surprise, she joined in as well. They were still laughing when the wine and appetizer arrived. He then ordered their actual meals before turning back to her.

"Here's to awkward silences and laughter at each other's expense," he toasted, raising his glass to her.

"And to memorable first dates," she added, raising her glass as well.

"First dates, you say? That implies there will be others. Look who's being presumptuous now," he teased.

"Do you want me to amend that or do you want to drink your damn wine?" she warned playfully.

He pressed the wine glass to his lips and drank from it, never taking his eyes off of Mackenzie. It was a challenge and she knew it. She considered her options carefully as she stared at him over the rim of her glass. With a sassy smirk and a raised eyebrow, she, too, drank to their toast.

"So, is this where we trade the 'where are you from' information of the night?" Nicolai asked, setting his glass down.

"In my opinion, the past can stay in the past. No real reason to know where we're from. I mean, we're obviously both from the south...let's just leave it at that." Mackenzie hoped that she had sounded nonchalant in her answer instead of nervous.

Instead, she turned his words back on him. "It's not like we're entering into a commitment, so it's all water under the bridge."

"Fair enough," he responded with a shrug. He could tell there was more to her story, something specific she didn't want him to know, but he also knew he wouldn't have to worry about her digging into his past either. "Let's try something safer, then. Favorite movie?"

The two fell into easy conversation after that and even easier banter. Mackenzie tried to pace herself on the wine before her, but was also thankful for the liquid courage. In another life, in another time, she could see herself really falling for him. Being in his presence was like catching up with a long-lost friend. It was comfortable, yet sassy and flirty.

When the server returned, she was surprised by the accuracy of Nicolai's choice for her entre. Still not knowing exactly what it was, she enjoyed it immensely and told him such. She couldn't believe he had guessed her tastes so accurately in such a short amount of time.

"I think we're disturbing the other guests," Mackenzie stated, trying to stifle her laugher at his most recent comment. She wasn't sure how long they had been there, but they were on their second bottle of wine.

"They probably should be disturbed. Your humor is as wicked as mine!" he replied with a smile. "And that is saying something!"

"Well, when you've been through what I've been through, it's bound to warp your sense of humor as well as a few other things," she admitted.

"And what would that be?" Nicolai questioned. His tone was casual, but his shoulders stiffened slightly.

"Ah...you're good," she said coyly, tipping her wine glass to him. "And with that, I am cut off. Where would I find the ladies room?"

"I'll go ahead and get the check. I'm sure we both have long days tomorrow," he offered as he pointed her in the right direction. While he was inwardly curious to know her story, her avoidance of his question didn't bother him. On the contrary, it seemed to raise his interest in her.

"Settle down boy," he muttered to himself.

He watched her walk away, her strut a little less steady than when they had arrived but still beyond sexy. She was impressively confident in her stilettos, telling him she wore them often, but she didn't seem one to work in an office setting. Pair that with the casual athletic gear she was wearing that morning and he was thoroughly confused. He knew there was a large prostitute operation in the area, but there was no way she was involved. Those ladies were basically schooled in how to play to a man's ego. Mackenzie definitely didn't fit that mold. She had shut him down so many times that night that he wasn't sure how he was still going.

He waved over the waiter as she left his line of sight and paid the bill, being sure to leave a generous tip for taking up their table for so long. He then decided to make his way over to the entrance and wait for her since it was right by the bathrooms. He figured it was the gentlemanly thing to do, not making her walk the extra steps just to repeat them in the opposite direction once more.

Mackenzie exited the bathroom, still checking her lip gloss. She noticed her date nearby and sucked in a steadying breath. She had obviously seen handsome men over the years, but he took the gold medal. Confidence radiated off of him, making him more attractive than looks alone could. Add that to his infuriatingly witty humor and it was a familiar mixture she hadn't had the chance to be near in ages.

She couldn't stop the smile from spreading across her face as she approached him if she had wanted to, and she wasn't sure she did. She hadn't been this relaxed in years and she was sure it had more to do with his easy-going attitude than the wine. He offered his arm to her once more and she gratefully accepted. A little indulgence while they walked to the car wouldn't hurt anything, right?

Playing the role of the perfect gentleman, he opened the passenger door for her when they reached the car.

"Wait," he instructed before she could sit down. "You seem to have something on your mouth."

Mackenzie thought back to the last look in the bathroom mirror. Had she missed something? Could this get any more embarrassing? Nicolai took her chin in his hand and gently turned her face one way, then the other. His other hand found its way to the small of her back, pulling her against him.

"What is it?" she asked, trying to focus with him so close.

"Me," he breathed.

Before she could process what he meant, his face lowered and his lips claimed hers as their own. Mackenzie stiffened at the intimate contact, but soon relaxed into him. The kiss was tender and unpressured, tame by most standards, but it didn't stop her mind from turning to mush.

As he pulled back, Mackenzie discovered that her hands had found their way to his very defined chest. She didn't recall doing that, but was in no way complaining. She could feel his heart racing beneath her fingertips, assuring her that she had not been the only one affected. Her own heart pounded in her ears and her breathing was not as calm as it had been moments earlier. Slowly, she opened her eyes she didn't remember closing and looked into his smiling face.

"You tricked me," he said playfully, a little out of breath himself.

"I what?" she questioned, trying to clear the fog in her head.

"You tricked me. I have all this sticky stuff on my lips now," he teased, using the back of his hand that had previously held her chin to wipe his mouth.

The motion just served to pull her attention back to his lips. She found herself staring at them, thinking of them pressed against hers once more. As they formed into a knowing smirk, she snapped herself out of her trance and pushed lightly against his chest. He provided minimum resistance as she stepped back.

"I have a disco ball's worth of glitter on my lips. I'm pretty sure you knew what you were getting yourself into," she retorted playfully, a little more breathless than she wanted to admit.

His smirk turned into a sheepish grin under the scrutiny of her blue eyes and he had the good sense to look, at least slightly, chastised.

"Guilty as charged," he confessed, helping her into the car. "I couldn't help myself."

Mackenzie smiled to herself as he rounded the end of the car. She hadn't been kissed at all in so long she had forgotten the rush that could accompany it. That had to be the reason her heart wouldn't slow and her hands still shook, not the man himself. She couldn't afford to let him close.

The rhythmic purr of the engine and soft sway of the car moving through traffic lulled them both into a peaceful silence on the ride back to Mackenzie's apartment. She wondered what he was thinking but was too shy to ask. She also wondered what was supposed to happen when they got to her place. They had already kissed, so the tension of do they or don't they was already less, but still she wondered.

It seemed like they arrived in the blink of an eye and Nicolai was opening her door, ever the gentleman, as he helped her step to the curb. Mackenzie smiled shyly as they reached her door. She searched through her clutch for her keys as her heart began to race once more.

"Would you like to come in for a night cap?" she asked before she lost her nerve.

His smile was slow and sexy as he motioned for her to go first. He followed her inside and she closed the door behind him, watching him carefully as Nicolai looked around the room. There was no judgement in his eyes, and she exhaled a breath she didn't know she had been holding.

She slipped past him and into the kitchen, acutely aware of his presence in her space. She reached above the sink to her alcohol cabinet and opened the door.

"What's your poison?" she asked without turning around.

Nicolai's strong hands gripped her hips from behind, eliciting a yelp of surprise. It quickly turned into a moan of desire as he pulled her back against him and began kissing his way down her neck to her shoulder.

Her besties voice rang through her head, urging her to have some fun. Taking her advice, she rolled her head to the other side, giving him easier access and giving in to the sensations he was evoking. He growled deep within his throat at her easy acceptance, the sound sending shivers throughout her body. She had neglected her body's urges for so long that it was overwhelming to finally give in.

He spun her around to face him and his mouth crashed down on hers. The kiss was vastly different from the first. Lust raged through them both, hot and demanding, as he urged her mouth open for his tongue to slip inside. His hands ran up the outside of her thighs to grip her ass, lifting her effortlessly into the air and placing her on the kitchen counter.

Her legs wrapped around his waist, raising her skirt with the motion and exposing her lacy panties. He pressed himself closer to her, his erection rubbing against her aching core making her squirm with the long unfamiliar need. His hands continued their upward path, this time taking her dress with it. She could feel the closely held restraint straining against his muscles, forcing himself to move slowly.

His mouth broke away from hers and he began kissing a path from her jaw to her collarbone, slowly and methodically driving her crazy with desire. His hands reached the top of her panties and crawled across the smooth skin of her abs.

"Jaxon," she exclaimed breathlessly as his fingers found the uneven, puckered flesh of her past.

Her eyes flew open in panic. Her mind was clouded with confusion and lust as she looked around frantically. The glow of streetlights and the dashboard were all that illuminated the space around her. She was still in his car. It was all a dream. The wine mixed with the motion of the car must have knocked her out.

She tried not to call attention to herself as she desperately tried to clear her head and act normal. His hands had felt so real, so intense. While that dream was miles above her normal nightmares, she would prefer not to have those while still in the man's car.

Nicolai sat as still as possible in the driver's seat. His jeans suddenly felt too tight as his arousal grew. This woman surprised him more than any woman before her and he couldn't seem to control his reactions to her. He hadn't been sure how to react when she fell asleep almost immediately after pulling into traffic, but that had been nothing compared to the soft noises she made in her sleep.

It was blissfully obvious what she was dreaming about and he was man enough to admit it had really revved his engine. He had even found himself having to 'adjust' several times as he tried to concentrate on driving. There was sure to be a cold shower in his future, but there was something else that piqued his curiosity more. He cleared his throat in preparation to ask.

"Who is Jaxon?"

Mackenzie felt like a bucket of ice water had been dumped over her. Any lingering sensations from the dream left immediately as Nicolai's question slammed into her. Dread rose within her as there was only one way for him to know that name.

"I...um...what?" she stammered, hoping beyond hope she had heard him wrong.

"You...um...apparently...talk in your sleep," he admitted, his voice huskier than it had been at dinner.

Mackenzie felt her face heating up with embarrassment. "Oh God," she whispered, wishing the ground would open up and swallow her whole.

"Please tell me I didn't..." she pleaded, letting her question drift off unfinished.

"Oh," he chuckled seductively. "You did." Even the surprise name couldn't dampen the desire running through him.

"That's it, I'm dead. I have died and gone to Hell," Mackenzie commented, trying not to dissolve into hysterics.

"Not likely, love," he assured her as his hand found its way to the inside of her knee.

"Whoa, okay, maybe you should just keep your hands on the wheel," Mackenzie insisted jumping away from his touch. Her heart leaped into her throat as she forced a glare at him. Just that slight contact was enough to send her over the edge.

"But really, who is Jaxon?" he asked again. Curiosity burning through him. Where did she know that name? Who was this woman really?

Mackenzie was filled with relief as her apartment came into view. She had her clutch firmly in her hand and was ready to leap from the car as it stopped at her sidewalk. His hand reached for her as her door swung open, but she easily avoided his grasp. She was already moving towards her apartment with his car door closed behind her when she heard him step out.

"Wait!" he called out.

"Thanks for dinner! I had a lovely time! I'm gonna go die now!" she called out, embarrassment refusing to let her turn around. "Probably not wise for you to walk me to the door, we...well...I already know how that ends apparently. Wait...shouldn't have said that. Anyway, I'm just gonna die once I get there!"

"I'll call you then?" he asked.

"Can't call someone who's dead!" she replied, fighting with the lock on her door.

"See you around," he laughed, still watching her.

"Doubtful!"

Finally, the door opened and she sprang through the entrance. Closing the door behind her, she leaned against it with a deflated groan.

"Good one," she told herself in the empty apartment. She pushed away from the door and headed for a much-needed cold shower.

Chapter 3

Mackenzie stepped out of her apartment and closed the door behind her. It was the first time she had stepped foot outside after the disastrous way her date had ended days before. Embarrassment had kept her locked away, even calling out of work, but she eventually had to face the world again. That included her bestie.

Reluctantly, she put her blue tooth head set on and dialed the familiar number.

"Mac! I was afraid he kidnapped you!" Jade exclaimed as preamble.

"Nope, but I'm going to have find a new coffee shop and maybe move out of the city if not the country," Mackenzie replied in defeat.

"Oh no! That bad? He had such promise!" Mackenzie heard Jade flop onto her bed.

"Oh no, the date was great...really great actually. Romantic dinner, sassy banter, didn't shy away from my brutal honesty and a nearly perfect gentleman. Even kissed me at his red sports car," Mackenzie highlighted.

"So...what happened?!" Jade gasped audibly as she put the pieces together. "Girl?! Did you get you some?"

"Er...only in my dreams...which just happened to be in his car...on the way home. I should never drink wine in public..." Even saying the words out loud made her want to crawl back in her hole of an apartment.

"Oh no...you didn't... you know you talk in your sleep, right?" Jade asked, shock dripping from her words.

"Yep...and now, so does he."

Jade dissolved into fits of laugher while Mackenzie glared at anyone she passed, picturing her best friends face on their head.

"Fuck you, Jade," Mackenzie stated dryly, no real malice in her voice.

Jade only laughed louder at her friend's obvious discomfort.

"Are you done yet?" Mackenzie asked, still glaring at random strangers. "There's more."

"Oh no, that's not all?" Jade tried desperately to pull herself together. Mackenzie could practically see her wiping the tears from her eyes. "Okay, okay, I'm ready."

"I may or may not have called out a name other than his," she admitted quietly.

"You WHAT?" Jade screeched. "You hussy! You've been holding out on me! Here I thought you were neglecting yourself and instead, you haven't been sharing the details!"

"No, it's not like that," Mackenzie swore. "It was Jaxon...I called for Jaxon."

"Jaxon?" Jade questioned, pausing her relentless teasing in confusion. "Jaxon, Jaxon? Like before-"

"Don't say that name," Mackenzie warned, cutting her bestie off. "Yes, that Jaxon."

"Why Jaxon? I thought you had gotten over him," Jade wondered.

"I had! At least, I thought I had," Mackenzie replied. "Something kept feeling familiar. Maybe just how easily we clicked. Maybe it was the banter back and forth, the way he seemed to like my sass. I don't know. He even used a phrase Jaxon used to use. Then, when he kissed me...I guess it all just reminded me of a ghost."

"Oh honey. Jaxon doesn't deserve you remembering him. He just up and left, vanished without so much as a 'kiss my ass' or 'fuck you'," Jade reminded her.

"I know, I really do. But it doesn't matter now. All that matters is that I have to find a new coffee shop, change my number, and move," Mackenzie counted them off on her fingers.

"Has he called you?" Jade asked, excitement back in her voice.

"And texted. I just ignore them. I'm too mortified to answer."

"Girl, seriously? You call him a different name and he still calls you back? What voodoo did you do to him?" Jade asked incredulously.

"I don't know, but again, it doesn't matter. There is no way I am seeing or talking to him again," Mackenzie swore. "But alas, I am at work."

"Fine, go be responsible. I'll just laugh at your misfortunes all night," Jade pouted.

The two friends said their good-byes and hung up the phone with Jade's laughter still ringing loud and clear. The sun was just setting as she stepped into the swanky nightclub. The lights were low, allowing a sense of privacy or romance, whichever the situation warranted. The feel had an old-world vibe, a time when organized crime ruled the city and jazz was first taking off. She was thankful the smoke was missing, however, that used to accompany such establishments.

She casually made her way to the employee lounge to put her bag away and get ready for the night. She was early, as usual, so she took her time and checked her reflection one last time in the mirror. Her makeup was similar to the night of her date, but the glittery lip gloss was replaced by a Hollywood red lipstick. Her hair was carefully pinned back in a low chignon, keeping it out of her face.

Her black pencil skirt hugged her hips and thighs and stopped just below her knees with the slit in the back rising just above her knee. Her top was well fitting as well, but it matched her lipstick in color. Her toned arms were bare and the V-neck neckline allowed enough skin to show for her not to get too hot, but not low enough to give anything away.

As she was about to leave the room, Elise, her boss and the one friend she had made in this town, came waltzing in. They shared a knowing look as Elise was only person beyond Jade who knew about the date. Mackenzie could feel her cheeks heating up already.

"Don't even..." Mackenzie warned. "Let's just get through tonight."

"My lips are sealed, as you say," Elise replied, giving a wicked smirk. "You harlot."

"Oh hush," Mackenzie chastised. She grabbed her apron and wrapped it around her waist before stepping out of the lounge.

Soft music played over the speakers and drinks clinked at the bar. She didn't have long to dwell on the embarrassment she felt as things picked up for the night. Patrons poured through the doors and almost every table was filled as alcohol flowed from the bar and food ran from the kitchen. Mackenzie was more than thankful for her well-worn shoes with as much as she was moving.

The night finally started to slow down as Elise motioned her over to the servers stand.

"I have a surprise for you," she began with a gleam in her eye.

"Oh, this should be good," Mackenzie sassed. "Lay it on me."

"There is a big party that just came in. All men, all high rollers. I thought to myself, 'Mac is gorgeous, she's our best, and a local favorite.' You'll be the best for this table. Besides, the tips will line your pockets and they aren't hard on the eyes," Elise wiggled her eyebrows suggestively.

"Oh goody," Mackenzie replied dryly.

"Go get 'em you hussy," Elise commented in an awkward mix of Italian and American accents.

"I'm going to stop teaching you American phrases," Mackenzie threatened. Elise's returning laughter followed Mackenzie as she made her way to the largest table in the club. In spite of herself, her friends humor brought a smile to her face.

Elise hadn't been lying, either. There wasn't a woman among them, and they were all varying degrees of handsome. As she neared the table, she put on her best smile and pulled out her southern girl charm.

"Hey boys, how are you doin' tonight?" she cooed at them.

The men looked on appreciatively and an incomprehensible reply circled the table, accompanied by head nods and smiles. She briefly scanned along each of the faces, not stopping long on any specific customer before she continued.

"Let's start with some drinks, shall we?"

She began moving around the table, treating each man as if he was the only one in the room. Her smile always dazzling and just a hint of flirty. Scotch. Whiskey. Brandy. Vodka. The range of drinks was as wide as the looks of the men themselves. She continued around the table until familiar green eyes stared back at her.

Nicolai tried to act as normal as he could as he came face to face with Mackenzie. This was the last place he expected to find her and the crowd he was with was not who he wanted her around. He tried to play it cool and hoped, in return, she would get the hint to follow his lead.

To her credit, she only broke character for half a second, not nearly long enough for the average person to notice. He casually ordered his drink and she moved along to the next person as if nothing was out of the ordinary. He was impressed by her poker face even as his heart pounded with the thrill of seeing her again. He had to find a way to speak to her away from the table.

Mackenzie finished taking the drink orders and made a hasty retreat to the bar. After the long task of putting so many orders into the POS system, she called her boss over.

"Elise!" the name came out as a whisper yell.

"Okay, don't kill me. I didn't know they were Mafia until after I sent you over," Elise began as she walked up.

"Mafia?!" Mackenzie squealed, trying desperately to keep the panic out of her voice.

"I know you have a steadfast rule against them, but seriously, look at where we are. This area is crawling with them. It was bound to happen eventually...and think of the tips," Elise pushed, trying to justify everything.

"It's worse than that," Mackenzie snapped, her anxiety skyrocketing. "Niko is with them! And if they are Mafia, then that means..."

"Niko is, too," Elise finished when Mackenzie didn't. "Oh, this is bad. At least you weren't planning on seeing him again anyway."

"Not. Helping," Mackenzie chastised. "A guy in the fucking Mafia knows where I live! Has my number! I had a dream about a man in the fucking Mafia!" She covered her face with her hands, leaving her greatest fear unspoken.

Nicolai watched Mackenzie across the lounge. He was thankful the men around him were in their own conversations and not paying him any attention. He felt, more than saw, the moment she learned who she was serving. He could sense the tension radiating off of her from across the room as she quietly yet forcefully voiced her disapproval. He didn't normally mind the stigma that went with his job, but she was different.

He watched her load drinks onto a tray and effortlessly carry it above her head to their table. From memory alone, she handed drinks out, getting each order correct and impressing many of the men with him. When she reached him, her smile never faltered, but she didn't quite meet his eyes either. He wanted to say something, anything, but lost his chance before she was gone to the next person.

"Hey Niko," Lorenzo began as he nudged him. "What is it with you Americans refusing to speak Italian? She thinks because she's hot that she can skate by." His words were fully in Italian and, he believed, unheard by anyone but Nicolai.

Before Nicolai had a chance to respond, the click-clack of heels against the tile floors interrupted him. He looked up to see blue eyes glaring at Lorenzo and a determined stance in her shoulders.

"Mi scusi signore, ma se preferisci posso passare all'italiano," she replied in beautiful Italian.

Nicolai struggled to keep a straight face at her offer to switch languages. He loved watching Lorenzo squirm under any circumstance, but it was even better when he had a front row seat to the feisty woman who had plagued his thoughts as well.

"I've found that men like it when I speak in English," she continued, changing back over to her native tongue. "They see it as exotic and…sexy. But if it's too *hard* for you…"

Nicolai lost his internal battle. His laugher rang out loud and proud at her sass and intended play on words. He knew she hadn't backed down from a challenge on their date, but even after freaking out at the knowledge of who these men were, she still wasn't willing to take shit from them. Mackenzie looked at him, finally, as Lorenzo sputtered to find a response, and winked before returning to her job.

Lorenzo puffed out his chest and muttered to himself, but Nicolai wasn't paying attention. His full focus was taken by the petite woman bustling around them, catering to their every whim. She never got flustered by their demands or looked overwhelmed. She fielded their advances like a pro, letting them all down gently. Once Lorenzo had his wits about him again, he even made a pass at her, much to Nicolai's aggravation. Again, she shut him down, but unlike the others, she did it in Italian to make sure he understood her.

"Maybe I should just take what I want," Lorenzo commented while she was at the other end of the table.

"No!" Nicolai responded before he could stop himself. It was more forceful than he would normally speak to his acquaintance and Lorenzo noticed it.

"Oh, you have a thing for her?" Lorenzo smirked, following Nicolai's gaze.

"Of course not. She's hot, but not my type," he lied, trying to put the other man off the trail.

"Well, then you won't mind if I..."

Mackenzie kept stealing glances at Nicolai as she went around the table. She knew he wanted to talk to her, she could feel it. Instead, she did everything she could to stay busy, completely unavailable. Then, something changed. His focus, almost the entire time, had been on her, yet suddenly, it was on the man to his right, the one she had schooled with her knowledge of the local language. Something seemed off as she moved to the next man at the table, taking orders.

His eyes met hers as she neared him and something similar to an apology flashed through his emerald greens. Before she could begin to figure out what he could be planning, Lorenzo stood up and started towards her with a Cheshire smile on his face. As he got closer, his hand extended towards her as she took a cautionary step back. Before he could touch her, though, he was suddenly pulled backwards, and Nicolai replaced him in her path.

"Trust me?" he questioned under his breath.

Confusion shot through her at his words. He knew she didn't trust him. She had told him that multiple times on their date. Why would he think it would be any different now, knowing what she knew?

He pulled her into his arms suddenly and his mouth was on hers. Her hand flew to his chest, intent on pushing him away, but something in the urgency of his kiss stilled her retreat. This kiss was different. It was as if he was staking his claim, protecting her even. His tongue teased her mouth open and swept inside. Everything about his grip on her and the insistence of his kiss was possessive in nature, urging her to comply.

Her mind turned against her, melting her body into his instead of pushing him away. She returned his kiss with a passion of her own. She gave an inch and he took the full mile, controlling everything about the encounter and she let him. She soaked up the attention he paid her and the power she held over him, relishing in the feel of his body responding to her touch.

When he broke off the kiss, they were both gasping for air. Her one hand was now twisted in his shirt instead of just against his chest, and her other hand had wound itself around his waist band. The other men at the table called out their approval of Nicolai's actions as the two of them stared at each other.

Reality hit her like a train as her hand at his back ran into the cold metal of a .45. Instinct kicked in without warning and the world around her slowed to a crawl. In one motion, the hand at his chest shoved him backwards while the one at his back wrapped around the handle of the firearm and pulled. Within seconds, she stood before him, gun cocked and loaded, pointed point blank at his chest. Her stance proved she was ready to fire at the first sign of movement.

A rustle at the table tried to draw her attention, but she stayed firm. Her eyes bored into Nicolai's, watching them go from confused to shock to...pride? He put his hands up in surrender, motioning for the others at the table, presumably ready to attack, to stand down.

"You touch me again, I'll put a hole in your chest," Mackenzie promised, no hint of teasing in her voice.

"Yes ma'am," Nicolai submitted with a smile, backing away. "Can I have my piece back?"

"I think I'll hang onto it, thanks. Call it an apology for taking liberties," she replied.

She glanced around the table, seeing approval on several faces. She tucked the gun in the waistband of her skirt and plastered a smile back on her face.

"Now, where was I?" she asked, slipping back into server mode and ignoring her racing heart.

She went through the motions, taking the rest of their orders like nothing had happened. On the inside, however, she was a total wreck. That kiss, their nearness, had affected her more than she wanted to admit. His rock-hard body pressed against hers was enough to short circuit her good sense to stay away.

And that kiss itself. It was all consuming, possessive. It was as if he was marking her, claiming her as his own and announcing to all that she was off limits to anyone else there. And it was hot. It had her body responding in ways it hadn't in years. That was going to be a problem.

He, beyond the embarrassment of the end of their date, was Mafia. Even if he wasn't officially part of them, he was still too close for comfort. The fact that he reminded her so strongly of a ghost from her past only served to confuse her more, and he definitely reminded her of Jaxon.

Jaxon was the last man to make her feel the way she currently did. Not even her ex-husband had such an effect on her, even in the beginning. Jaxon, and now Nicolai, could make butterflies take flight in her stomach with just a look. Nicolai's touch felt so much like Jaxon that it was devastating to her entire being.

That familiarity had to be the reason he had such an effect on her. He pulled at memories of a lifetime ago, a better time that was stolen from her. Nicolai, and his Mafia connection, meant nothing more than a memory. At least, that was what she told herself as she walked over to the lounge and off the floor.

"What the hell was that?" Elise questioned, bombarding her as she entered the room.

"That was Niko, and I'm not entirely sure," Mackenzie admitted. She flopped down on the couch unceremoniously.

"He kissed you!" Elise exclaimed.

"He sure did," Mackenzie agreed wistfully, her fingers touching her lips absentmindedly.

"And you pulled a gun on him!" Elise yelled.

"Yep," Mackenzie replied quietly.

"Where did you get a gun?" her boss asked, looking at the tightness of her clothing.

"I took his from him," Mackenzie confessed, a little more confidently.

"You what?! You took his...what are you going to do now?" Elise squeaked, her voice low as to not be overheard.

"I'm going to grab their food from the kitchen and deliver it to the table and I am going to finish out my night." She stood up and smoothed out her skirt. Then she walked to the mirror and checked her lipstick, thankful for her 'all day stay' lipstick, and she walked to the door.

"You are going to act like nothing happened?" Elise called out to her.

"Yep."

Nicolai watched as Mackenzie returned from the back of the club. Her head was held high and a determined strength was in her shoulders. As she turned towards the kitchen, light reflected off of his gun in the small of her back, bringing a smirk to his face.

She had help this time as she carried a tray over to their table. Another beautiful woman carried a tray for half of the table. This one had black hair in more of a pixie cut, a little longer on one side than the other and was a few inches shorter than their official server. She was dressed similarly to Mackenzie, but the choice of footwear was drastically different. Where Mackenzie strutted around in stilettos that had a slightly pointed toe, her companion wore combat boots.

He was amazed, as he turned his attention back to Mackenzie, at her ability to continue as if nothing out of the ordinary had happened. He, on the other hand, was still shifting in his seat to hide his discomfort. Never in his life had he been more aroused by a gun being pointed at him, but he had never had his own gun drawn on him by a beautiful woman.

"Mac, can I get a refill on my drink?" he found himself asking as she came closer. He couldn't seem to leave her alone.

"I think you've had enough tonight," she replied with one eyebrow raised. "And it's Mackenzie, if you don't mind."

"I just assumed a woman as confident as you would have an equally confident nickname," Nicolai replied, back peddling to hide their previous connection.

"Maybe I do, but that would be outside of work only, and I don't see us having a need to meet outside of my job," she answered, giving him a pointed look.

Nicolai laughed out loud at what she was inferring. He couldn't seem to help himself when it came to her and it seemed that she was in the same boat. Their combined inability to keep their conversations devoid of sass was going to prove an issue before long. The others at the table had already been giving him a hard time about her taking his .45.

Mackenzie leaned seductively across him suddenly, stealing his breath away. He sat back slightly, his eyes bulging as he attempted to comprehend what was going on. Slowly, she stood back up, a smug look on her face as she winked at him.

"Buon appetite," she smirked, looking down at him.

His brows furrowed as he looked at her. He finally pulled his eyes away from her and glanced at the table. A chuckle bubbled up inside him as he realized what had just happened. She had placed his food in front of him. It had all been a way to prove an unspoken point to him. He looked away from his entre only to find that she had already moved on.

"Are you okay, friend?" Lorenzo asked, nudging him sharply.

"Peachy," Nicolai responded lightly.

By the time the end of the meal rolled around, Nicolai was practically jittery with anticipation. He paid his tab with the other server that had helped Mackenzie earlier and waited as patiently as he could. He said good-bye to each of the other men at the table and made his way to the server's station. Once he was sure the rest of the party had left, he caught the server's attention.

"Can I help you?" the woman with the 'Elise' name tag asked.

"Is there any way I could speak to Mac for a second," he asked, his eyes searching the club for her.

"Sorry friend," Elise began sadly. "She left ten minutes ago. Better luck next time."

Nicolai stared at her incredulously. She had given him the slip.

Chapter 4

Mackenzie soaked up the sun the next morning at the local beach, glad she decided to take another morning off from her gym routine and just relax and recharge. She would forever be thankful to Elise for letting her escape out the back door the previous night before the check was paid. It was obvious that Nicolai wanted to talk to her, and after the text from Elise confirming her suspicions, she was even happier her boss had worked with her.

She knew there was a possibility, now that he knew where she worked, that he would show back up tonight. That had been the biggest reason she decided to go to the beach. The sounds of the crashing waves of crystal-clear water and the warmth of the sand and sun always calmed her. She needed all the help she could get if she was going to see him again. Just the sight of him seemed to send her hormones into overdrive now, especially after that kiss. If the look on his face was any indication, if that kiss hadn't done something for him, the flirtatious way she had delivered his food definitely had.

She smiled to herself as she remembered the look on his face. She could still feel his eyes following her as she walked away. After his little stunt with the kiss, turnabout was fair play.

"Is that smile for me?"

Mackenzie's smile melted off her face as the male voice reached her ears. A shadow slid over her and her heart started to race.

"I guess you came for your gun?" she asked, eyes still closed. She hoped she looked much calmer than she felt.

"Nah, keep it. It looks better on you than it does on me," Nicolai confessed, his grin heard through his voice.

"Good, 'cuz I left it at home," she retorted.

"I would have figured you for the bikini type. Or the 'no lines' approach. You definitely have the body for it," he commented.

"I prefer not to give everything away with one look," she dodged, finally opening her eyes to look at him. Her mouth went dry at the vision before her. He was in swim trunks only. The muscles she had guessed were beneath his clothes were gloriously on display with just a hint of sweat glistening across them. Her eyes couldn't help but wander over that V as it dipped below the waistband of his boardshorts.

"See something you like?" he asked knowingly.

"Oh...I do," she admitted. "But looks aren't everything."

"What is that supposed to mean? Are you embarrassed by that dream you had in my car?" he wondered, his smile growing to overtake his already dangerously attractive face.

"Of course!" Mackenzie scoffed, her face flushing at the thought. "But beyond that, your choice of acquaintances is a total no go."

"Lorenzo? He's harmless, mostly," he replied, playing dumb.

"Mafia. Not just Lorenzo, although I did have fun poking that bear," she admitted. "By the way, you're blocking the sun, so move to the side, would ya?"

"Of course, Your Highness," he mocked, moving to sit beside her. "And as far as the Mafia goes, I'm not-"

"Doesn't matter," she interrupted. "I don't need an explanation. The affiliation is close enough, so if I wasn't out before, I definitely am now."

"You realize where you work, right? Where you live? It may not be their official territory, per say, but it's not far from it," he informed her, assuming she didn't know.

"Yes, I know. I'm close enough to danger for it to shield me without burning me in the process," she answered, revealing more than she meant to.

He studied her carefully, his eyes narrowing at her. "Who or what are you hiding from?"

"Is there a reason you are here, Niko?" she questioned, dodging his as she looked away.

"You wouldn't answer my calls, my texts. I wanted to see you," he told her, dropping it for now.

"Maybe I didn't want to see you," she retorted, shooting him a look out of the side of her eye.

"Of course you did. If not, why would you have flirted with me so much last night?" he challenged.

"Maybe I was just doing my job...better tips and all that," she countered, closing her eyes. Even behind her sunglasses, she didn't want to take the chance of him seeing the truth behind her words.

"Shutting down Lorenzo was doing your job. Being polite yet sassy was doing your job. That move with my gun and then my food...that was above and beyond," he stated, calling her bluff. "And that kiss...damn."

"I didn't need them thinking I was an easy target. Anyway, how did you know I wouldn't pull the trigger?" She sat up to look at him, ignoring the comment about the kiss, the one that still sent shivers through her.

A slow smile crept along his face and he lowered his sunglasses to look at her. "When someone has a dream like that about you on a first date, they aren't likely to kill you the next time you see them, even if they did call you by the wrong name."

Mackenzie looked out over the sea, unable to sit still under the scrutiny of his emerald green eyes.

"Besides, you left the safety on."

"I did that on purpose. I guess you're right, I didn't want to kill you," she admitted as she turned back to him. A mischievous smile crossed her face. "Too public. Too many witnesses. And a gun? Too much blood all over me for being so close. No thanks."

His laughter warmed her more than the Mediterranean sun could ever hope to as she laid back down.

"You are one hell of a woman," Nicolai commented once he stopped laughing. "Which is why I find myself drawn to you."

"Too bad. Like I've already said, your affiliation with the Mafia is a hard pass for me. Sorry, not sorry." She felt more like she was convincing herself more than him. The sound of the waves filled the silence that stretched between them.

"Don't go to work tonight," he finally said, moments later.

"What?" Mackenzie couldn't believe what she was hearing. "Why not? And I swear to God if you say to trust you, so help me."

"I'll explain later, just don't go to work tonight." The teasing tone she had come to expect from him was gone, he was all business and something about that resonated within her.

"Fine, I won't go," she conceded.

"I'm serious. I'll pay you what you'll lose in tips, I'll-"

"I said I won't go. I mean it," she huffed, cutting him off. "And I don't need your money."

"You're serious..." he said skeptically.

Mackenzie rolled her eyes and grabbed her phone. She quickly pulled up the number for Elise and hit send. After a few rings, the line answered, and she immediately started talking. "Hey Elise. I know I owe you one...or two...or ten, but I need another favor. I'm not coming in tonight. I'm..." She gave a dramatic yet obviously fake cough, "sick. No, I'll be fine, just won't make it in...thanks."

She put her phone away and gave him a pointed look.

"Happy?"

"Good. Well, I'd love to stay and chat, but I have to go get ready for a meeting. I'll catch you later," he suggested as he stood up and brushed the sand off of himself.

"Yeah, good luck with that," she called out as he walked away, confused at his sudden departure. His laugher drifted away the further he got, leaving just the sounds of the sea once more.

***

Nicolai sat at the same table he had sat at the night before. Lorenzo, as usual, sat next to him and was on the verge of talking his ear off. Nicolai tried to keep up with the forced conversation, but his mind was racing. He checked his watch again for the umpteenth time.

"You have a date tonight or something?" Lorenzo asked, catching onto his nervous habit.

"No, of course not. I was just wondering where the waitress is. I'm thirsty and we've been waiting for 15 minutes already," he lied, looking around the lounge.

"Oh, thirsty? Or are you looking for that sweet piece of ass from last night?" Lorenzo guessed, amusement lacing his voice.

"I think she made it clear to everyone here that she was off limits," Nicolai warned, trying to keep his co-worker off that trail of thought. "Besides, she still has my gun."

"Oh, you're afraid of her, is that it?" Lorenzo poked.

"A broad who isn't afraid of stealing a man's gun and using it against him in a room full of Mafia? I'd say that's one bad ass bitch. Probably not wise to get on her bad side," Nicolai suggested, looking directly at Lorenzo.

"Nah, probably not, but she sure would be fun."

Nicolai fisted his hands by his sides, willing himself from punching the other man. He found himself being oddly protective of Makenzie and tried to push it off as common curtesy. He didn't have time for anything beyond that. Before he could think much further on the subject, Elise walked over to the table and introduced herself as their server for the night.

"She's not here," she stated knowingly as she reached Nicolai. "She called out...again."

"What a shame," he lied. "I hope she's okay. Is she sick?"

"I don't think she wants any soup or a get well soon card from you if that's what you're thinking," Elise shot back.

"Actually, I was afraid she might be contagious," Nicolai joked. "We did kiss last night. Swapping bodily fluids and all."

Elise narrowed her eyes at him. "About that. You pull a stunt like that again and I'll have you hauled out of here by your ears, understood?"

"Yes ma'am," he replied, raising his hands in surrender. "Who would have known they hid all the beautiful but crazy women in the city in this club?"

"Watch it buddy," she warned. She gave him another pointed look, like there was more she wanted to say but didn't, before continuing down the table.

The table was longer tonight as more of the crime family had decided to join after hearing about the entertainment from the previous night. The second in command had even decided to grace them with his presence. Elise finally made it through everyone's orders and made her way to the bar to have drinks made that would never make it to the table.

"Five minutes," a voice whispered in his ear over the well-hidden communicator.

Nicolai checked his watch and set an internal timer. He reminded himself to play it cool, to act as if nothing was out of the ordinary. He had worked too long for this to blow it now.

He went through the motions of seemingly being part of the conversations around him. A nod here, a chuckle there, as if this night was just like any other. On the inside, though, he was mapping the room, noting where all those working there were stationed, finding all the exits.

He checked his watch again. Two minutes. He took a deep, steadying breath as he waited. He was thankful Mackenzie had agreed to call out and kept her word. She was a distraction he didn't need tonight.

"Breaching in 10...9...8...7..." The countdown sounded in Nicolai's earpiece as Elise began stacking drinks on a tray. As the voice reached one, several doors around them flew open and officers in all degrees of protective gear came filing in the room. Shouting filled the air as chaos reigned around them. Everyone, including Nicolai, stood at the table, drawing their weapons. He saw Elise duck behind the bar for cover.

"Polizia! Scendere!" rang through the room, commanding everyone to get down.

A shot sounded and Nicolai noticed the second in command was fighting against the police.

As the rest of the force began closing ranks, Lorenzo slipped away. Nicolai searched the faces of the officers until he found who he was looking for. A silent question passed between them, followed by an almost invisible nod.

"Make it look good," he mumbled as he turned and went after Lorenzo.

He had hoped that tonight was his last night with these low lives, but it seemed Lorenzo had other plans. As he ran the direction he had seen the other man flee, a shot hit the wooden door frame beside his head, splintering the wood and showering it down around him.

"Damn it, Bertotti, I said make it good, not kill me," he grumbled as more shots were fired around him.

He finally caught up to Lorenzo as he was escaping through the kitchen. He ran with him, intent on keeping his cover intact. They burst out the kitchen door into the still young night and sprinted to Lorenzo's car. They both jumped inside and the car sprang to life.

"Where to?" Lorenzo questioned.

"I met with Francesco and rode with him. My car is a couple blocks away. You can drop me there," Nicolai told him.

"You think it's safe to go to your car?" Lorenzo challenged, smelling that something wasn't right.

"I can't just leave it for them to find and then track me. I have to take that chance," Nicolai fibbed, staying to character.

"True, I suppose you're right."

Nicolai gave directions as Lorenzo drove. It wasn't long before they had arrived at the little red sports car.

"What about you? Where are you going?" Nicolai asked before stepping out.

"He needs to know. I am not sure who else got away, so I can't assume he has already found out," Lorenzo informed him.

"Fair enough. I'm going to lay low for a few days. Let the heat die down. Let me know if you hear anything."

Nicolai closed the door behind him as he exited the car. He waited until Lorenzo drove away before letting out a frustrated breath. He knew takedowns didn't always go as planned, but this was ridiculous. He had been on this case for four years, trying to get enough dirt to have them where they wanted them. Tonight was supposed to be it. Maybe one more raid to get the head honcho, but his daily involvement was supposed to be over.

"Damn it!" he shouted to the empty parking lot, running his hands through his hair.

He slid into the driver's seat of his car and pulled out a cell phone that had been taped under the steering wheel. He hit the send button and called the last known number.

"Haier, glad you called," the voice on the other end began immediately.

"How did it go?" Nicolai questioned, frustration evident in his voice.

"Could have been worse. We rounded up most of them, but three, besides you, got away. Any idea where Lorenzo was heading?" the voice asked.

"He said he was going straight to the top like the good little lap dog he is," Nicolai replied dryly.

"Shit. He won't leave there anytime soon and we both know the Don will lock everything down tight." He paused. "I know you hate this..."

"Yeah...I know...I'm still in," Nicolai spat.

"Just lay low. If they reach out to you, we'll be there. If not, you have a quiet little vacation."

"Yeah, yeah, yeah...I can find ways to occupy my time," Nicolai sighed. Mackenzie's face popped into his head and he pushed it away. "And Bertotti, you almost shot me."

"No, I didn't. I knew right where that bullet was going. I'm a great shot!" Bertotti protested.

"Sure you are...just be careful. I don't really feel like dying by friendly fire," Nicolai huffed.

"Yeah yeah...don't be such a baby," Bertotti joked, his laugh cutting through the line.

Nicolai grumbled out a 'good-bye' and hung up the phone. He scrubbed his hands over his face and slammed them into the steering wheel.

"Fuck!" his voice filled the small loaner car. Sometimes he wondered who was worse, the Mafia scum he was trying to get off the streets, or the police agencies assigned to be his backup.

He knew they wanted him to go 'home' and stay put, out of sight out of mind and all that. They wanted him ready to jump at any moment if Lorenzo or the others called him. He also knew he wouldn't sleep until he knew that a certain brunette was, in fact, safe from all this.

He turned the car on and the engine roared to life. He found himself directing the car in the opposite direction of his current living quarters and towards Mackenzie's instead. He was beyond telling himself that he was going for professional curtesy. Every fiber of his body needed to see her, to talk to her. Hell, he really even wanted to hear that borderline bitchy sass that always seemed to flow from her perfect mouth.

Traffic was light tonight as he cruised through the city streets. Which was good, since his thoughts were firmly planted on her and the way everything she did affected him. There had only ever been one other woman to take over his senses like she did. Fiona.

Fiona had been a red headed spit fire who could cut through his bullshit faster than anyone else. She had been his entire world at one time. They were going to get married before the universe decided it had different plans. That had to be why he was so drawn to Mackenzie. Her personality was an almost exact match to Fiona's. A little more jaded, a little less trusting, but still close enough to bring back memories. As far as looks, Fiona had been beautiful, but Mackenzie had something that Fiona didn't. Where Fiona was soft and slender, Mackenzie was muscled, toned, and curvy. The only real similarities between them, were the freckles and their height.

As he pulled up outside of her apartment, he stared at her window. His resolve strengthened. He may still be undercover, but it was almost over. He still needed his cover, but he couldn't stand the loathing in her eyes when she thought he was actually with them. He was going to tell her the truth, maybe not all of the truth, but at least that he was undercover. The rest could come later.

He jumped out of his car and jogged up to her door. A smile found its way to his face as he knocked. He wondered if she would threaten to shoot him again. He found the thought oddly arousing as he waited. He knocked again when there was no answer.

Several seconds and no noise inside later, he began to feel panic rising within him. He hated what he was about to do, again, but he had to. He pulled out his phone and pulled up an app. Punching her number in, he wanted for the tracking software to find her.

His blood ran cold when it dinged with her location. She wasn't home.

***

Mackenzie made her way through the throng of people as everyone gathered in Piazza del Duomo. Thousands of people had descended upon the Sicilian city for Festa di Sant'Agata, the festival that celebrated the martyrdom of the city's patron saint, Saint Agatha. There was music, food, fireworks, and a procession during the three-day festival. Some people came for the deeply spiritual side of things, others for the ambiance of the festival itself. Mackenzie fell into the latter, wanting to know what it was all about. Since she promised Nicolai she wouldn't go to work for whatever reason, she found herself with time to attend.

The pedestrian area of the city was filled to the max with festival goers and activities. Food and drinks were pouring through the streets with the late-night cafes and bars, not to mention street venders that showed up for the masses. Mackenzie stuck to nonalcoholic drinks tonight for two reasons: a. crazy people around her were already going to be drinking, and

b. the situation the wine got her into last time. Falling asleep and having sexy dreams in someone else's car was not in her future any time soon.

The fireworks were set to begin soon, so she followed the herd of people with her pizza and coke, eager to see them for herself. She was on her own, as usual, wishing she could share this with her bestie. They had always traveled together in their youth. Germany, Austria, you name it. Being at the festival without her brought up old memories, and with it, old pain.

Family she would never see again. A love lost. Friends she had left behind. An entire existence gone in the blink of an eye with no hope of returning. A solitary life was to be her fate now. She suddenly felt completely alone in the sea of people. She took a long swallow of her drink, vowing to have something stronger once she got home.

After a few more minutes of self-loathing, she squared her shoulders and took a deep breath. There was nothing she could do about it right now. Instead, she was determined to enjoy her night at a festival she had never experienced before. She pushed all negative thoughts aside and took a bite of her pizza.

The hot cheese, Italian seasonings, and delectable toppings hit her taste buds in an explosion of flavor. She closed her eyes in appreciation and savored the moment. Despite her sobering memories, she smiled to herself. She was in the land of Italian food, pristine beaches, and warm weather. Who could stay sad in a place like that?

As she opened her eyes, something large and off balance slammed into her, sending her sprawling to the ground. She landed with an unceremonious thud and a groan that could be heard over the blasting music. Looking around to gather her bearings, she found her pizza and coke spilled next to her and an obviously drunk man standing over her.

"Great," she mumbled to herself.

"My bad, let me help you," the man slurred.

"How do I keep finding all the freaking Americans lately?" Mackenzie asked herself quietly as he hoisted her to her feet.

"Dude, how did I get so lucky?" the giant wondered, swaying on his feet.

"Lucky?" she questioned, not sure how her being ran over by a freight train made him lucky.

"Yeah man, you speak English and you're hot!" the frat boy wannabe commented.

"I'm not even going there," Mackenzie muttered as she turned to walk away.

"Hey!" he called out. "Where are you going?"

"Away from here," she huffed, not slowing her steps. "Maybe to replace my pizza. Or drink."

"Aren't you going to thank me?" His words stopped her short, almost sending him careening into her once more.

"Thank you? For running over me?" she scoffed, turning back to him.

"For helping you up, of course," he told her, grinning like an idiot.

"I wouldn't have needed you to help me up if you hadn't run over me in the first place," she reminded. "So, are you going to apologize for running me over?"

"Oh, that was an accident." He looked appalled that she would ask such a thing.

"Right. I guess that's your answer on my show of gratitude." Mackenzie turned on her heel and started through the crowd.

A hand wrapped around her arm and pulled her to a stop once more. Her eyes stared at the offending appendage and then into the eyes of the human attached to it. Her eyebrow raised in question.

"Let me take you to dinner," he offered.

"Let go of me," she countered.

"We're both tourists-"

"I'm not a tourist."

"- and I'm sure we could explore the city together," he continued as if she hadn't commented.

"Let go of me," she repeated firmly.

"Oh, come on, don't be that way," he begged.

Mackenzie blocked out his voice as she reached for her collapsible baton in the small of her back with her free hand. With a flick of her wrist, it extended behind her, ready to use.

"You have five seconds-"

Before she could finish her threat, the hand was ripped from her arm and there was another large, more imposing body between her and her would-be date.

"If you know what's best for you, I suggest you take off."

Chapter 5

Mackenzie stood there staring at Nicolai's back as he, she assumed, glared at the drunkard. She couldn't help but admire the way his cotton t-shirt stretched nicely over his muscled back and shoulders. His jeans were slung low on his hips, drawing her gaze to his well-defined rear.

"Go," he growled, snapping her out of her visual inspection.

The other man had the good sense to know he was in serious danger of getting his ass kicked and took off. Mackenzie giggled as Nicolai turned back to her. He, however, did not look amused. He looked mad enough to throttle her.

"What are you doing here?" he questioned.

"I could ask you the same question," she countered, more than a little put off by his irritation at her.

"Mac," he warned.

"It's a festival. What do you think I'm doing here?" she scoffed.

"What the hell was that?" he asked, pointing to where the frat boy had been.

"I had it handled. I can take care of myself," she reminded him.

"I told you to stay home," he stated, frustration laced through his voice.

"No, you told me not to go to work. That is not the same as 'stay home'. What's the big deal anyway?"

"What's the big d – seriously? What's the..." he paused and took a deep breath before steering them both into a quiet alleyway. "Do you know where I was tonight?"

"How would I know where you were? Wait...for that matter, how did you know where to find me?" Her eyes narrowed on his and her hands flew to her hips.

Nicolai stopped cold. She had caught him. He needed to calm down and take a breath before continuing on. She was not who he was mad at and it wasn't fair to her that he was taking it out on her.

"Well?!" she pressed when he didn't answer.

He was dumbfounded, speechless. The anger radiating from her only proved to make her more beautiful. The scent of her shampoo teased his nose and made him painfully aware of how closely they were standing. Her low-cut tank top gave him the perfect view of her more than ample breasts while her short blue jean shorts showed off her toned, freckled legs. Even the extended night stick in her hand made her irresistibly sexy.

"Are you following me?!" Mackenzie was over it. What was his deal? He was staring at her like a crazy person.

'A hot crazy person,' she thought to herself. She shook her head to clear the thought.

"Let me start over," he finally stated apologetically. "I'm sorry, I know you had that guy handled. Somehow, I probably saved him more than I saved you." He looked pointedly at the night stick.

Mackenzie deflated slightly, appeased by his words. "Thank you," she replied, collapsing her nightstick against the wall. "I'm not some damsel in distress."

"I know that," he chuckled. "And I'm sorry. It's not you that has me pissed. There was a raid tonight, at the club you work at, and then you weren't home. I was worried something had happened to you."

"Wait...what?" She had been mesmerized by his too kissable lips, but was suddenly snapped out of it. "A raid? At the club? Is that why you didn't want me going to work?"

"Yes, there was a raid-" he began, but was cut off.

"If there was a raid, with police, how are you here?" she wondered. Her mind raced with possibilities.

"How do you think?" he questioned, ready to see the relief in her eyes when she put the pieces together.

"Oh my God...you...you escaped?!" she screeched.

"What?" He couldn't believe it. She had put the pieces together, but in all the wrong way.

"So, not only are you with the Mafia, but now you're on the run from the police?"

"No! Nothing like-"

"Of course not...you probably bought the police. You're with the freaking Mafia. That's probably how you knew to warn me about the raid," she surmised, drawing her own conclusions.

"Whoa...no...I-"

"I can't believe this! I find one hot guy who I actually kinda like-"

"Kinda?"

"-and not only is he in the Mafia, but running from the fucking police. Not again...not this time."

"Again? What does that mean?" Nicolai asked, obviously there was more going on than he knew.

"I can't do this." She started moving away from him. She needed air and to remove herself from his intoxicating presence.

"Wait! Let me explain! It's not what you think!" he tried to tell her, but she was already shutting down.

"I have to go. Do. Not. Follow. Me!" She punctuated her words carefully.

Before he could stop her, she was gone. She had slipped into the crowd of festival goers and used them to disappear. Nicolai exhaled a frustrated breath and ran his hand through his hair.

"Well, that went well."

***

Natural light met her eyes as she stepped out of the metal box. Executive floor. Owners suites. Only the best for the privileged men and women on this floor. Her smile faltered a bit as, again, the usually bustling hall was devoid of all human presence. Just as before, she pushed the uneasiness aside. Not today.

As she reached her intended door, she paused once more. Breathing deeply to steady her shaking hands, she renewed the smile on her face and ran her free hand through her copper-red hair. Exhaling her held breath, she opened his door and stepped inside with more confidence than she suddenly felt.

"Oh Lawrence, honey! I know you hate when I don't call ahead," she called out in a sing-song voice. "But I was in the area and decided to grab lunch!" She continued through the outer office to his private area in the back. Hearing his voice, she opened the inner door. "Lawre-"

Her words were cut off by a quiet popping noise and what sounded like a bag of bricks being dropped on the floor. Four men, not including her husband, stood around what appeared to be a crumbled man in a cheap suit laying on the ground. In her husband's hand was a literal smoking gun, a silencer attached to the end.

The bag of take-out clattered to the tile floor as shock overtook her body. Her eyes widened to the point of being painful and blood rushed to her ears. She stared at the body on the floor, trying to create a rational scenario in her muddled mind that didn't involve her husband shooting it dead. Her mouth hung open and an audible gasp escaped her lips.

***

Mackenzie stood slumped over her bathroom counter. Her hands firmly pressed into the solid surface, holding herself upright while her head hung in defeat. She tried to take deep, steadying breaths, willing the nightmares out of her mind. Her body still shook from the lingering images.

"Mac? Are you still with me?" Jades voice called out. The cell phone sat on the counter on speaker phone.

"Yeah, I'm here," Mackenzie answered softly.

"Talk to me," Jade coaxed. "Are you still having nightmares?"

"Yep...you could say that," Mackenzie stated flatly.

"How often?"

Mackenzie scrubbed a shaky hand over her face. "Every time I close my eyes. Day. Night. Doesn't matter."

"Jesus," Jade whispered. "How much sleep are you getting?"

"Three, four hours if I'm lucky," Mackenzie admitted. "But it's never restful. They are always there."

"Have you tried talking to someone about this?"

"I thought that's what we were doing, Jade." She grabbed a washcloth from under the counter and soaked it in cold water before pressing it to her face.

"I meant a professional. Someone who knows how to handle PTSD," Jade clarified.

Mackenzie mumbled incomprehensibly from behind the washcloth.

"Sorry Mac, didn't catch that."

"I said, I can't exactly do that," she repeated, uncovering her face. "How exactly would I answer the questions when they started? What was happening in your life at the onset of these episodes? Are these memories? No...too easy to track me that way."

"Right, I didn't think about that."

The line went quiet as they sat lost in their own thoughts. Mackenzie began the long process of putting her long, thick red hair up into a braid that was as flat as possible. She then reached behind her and grabbed her brown wig, carefully positioning it on her head so that no red peeked through. Next to the sink was a contact case. She popped in the blue colored contacts and pulled her brunette hair into a bun. She looked at the stranger in the mirror and heaved a heavy sigh.

"You look like someone else again," Jade guessed.

"Yep," Mackenzie confirmed, pulling on her workout gear.

"I just thought about something!" Jade exclaimed, hope filling her voice. "You don't ALWAYS have nightmares. A certain someone inspires a different kind of dream."

"Oh...right," Mackenzie cringed. "About that. I forgot I haven't talked to you since then."

"What happened?"

"I have horrible taste in men. Like...the worst," she began, grabbing her gym bag.

"I mean, Lawrence was a *real* winner, but I thought things went great with Niko?" Jade commented, confused.

"Well, that asshole started out great, too, if you remember," Mackenzie retorted.

"Meh...mediocre at best. I always knew you were settling. After Jax left, you kinda deflated. I always assumed you married that asshole out of spite," Jade admitted. "He never liked our jokes. And we are freaking hilarious!"

"Anyway...Niko showed up at my work the other night," Mackenzie began, exiting her house and stepping out into the sunshine. She held her phone to her ear now. "He...um...he kissed me in front of an entire table of men."

"What?" Jade gasped, happy squeals piercing the line. "What did you do?!"

"I...um...pulled a gun on him..."

"I'm sorry...you what?!" Jade shrieked. "Please tell me you are joking?"

"Nope...and I don't even wish I could," Mackenzie chuckled walking down the street.

"Why? And better yet, where did you get the gun?"

"It was his. I took it out of his waist band while we kissed."

"Why did he have a gun? And why did you use it on him?" Jade asked frantically.

"Well...you see...the men at that table were part of the Mafia. I didn't need them getting the wrong idea about me," Mackenzie admitted.

"Ah, I guess that makes sense," Jade agreed. "Wait...all of them were Mafia?"

"Yep. All of them."

"But that means..." Jade couldn't finish the thought out loud.

"Yep."

"Damn it!"

"Oh, believe me, I know," Mackenzie murmured. "But it gets worse."

"Lay it on me," Jade replied resolutely.

"He showed up at the beach the next day. Told me not to go to work that night. For some stupid reason, I agreed. Maybe I just didn't want to risk running into him again. I don't know. Anyway, I went to a festival instead. He then shows up at the festival and tells me there was a raid and he got away!"

"I mean, that's good, right?"

"You're not thinking this through, Jade. A raid to take down the Mafia. He got away. Not only is he with the freaking Mafia, but now the police are actively looking for him!"

"And will look into anyone near him," Jade sighed, putting the pieces together. "What are you going to do?"

"I don't know." Mackenzie's shoulders slumped. "I may have to move again."

"You really liked this guy, didn't you?" Jade asked knowingly.

"I mean, he reminded me of Jax. Easy to talk to, easy to joke with. Really *really* easy on the eyes. And he just had this way of making me feel..."

"Excited? Wanted? Nervous? Tingly? Feisty? I can keep going," Jade joked.

"All those things...and safe. It's been a hell of a long time since I've felt safe," Mackenzie admitted.

"And now you've lost that again. Fuck." Jade went quiet for a moment. "I always try to imagine you happy and safe, ya know? It makes it easier to be apart."

"And I generally try to help you keep that image," Mackenzie confessed.

"Okay...okay...new plan," Jade announced, pulling herself from the gloom that had overtaken the conversation. "A date got us into this mess, and a date will get us out of it."

"Us? I'm pretty sure it's all me, here. And I can't go on another date with him. Fucking. Mafia."

"Now who's not thinking?" Jade countered. "A date with someone else! Anyone else! Maybe it's not just this guy you can't have! Maybe, it's the idea of no longer being on your own that you love!"

"That is the worst idea I have ever heard!" Mackenzie scoffed.

"No, really though!" Jade pushed.

"I don't usually date random people. The last one turned out sooooo great," Mackenzie reminded her. "And I don't exactly like my male coworkers enough to ever do that."

"Come on!"

"What am I supposed to do, find some random guy on the street and be like 'hey... you... me... dinner... tonight... your treat... that café around the corner at 7 pm. Don't be late'?" Mackenzie asked mockingly.

"Yes!" Jade exclaimed.

"Yes," a strange male voice answered at the same time.

"Who was that?" Jade asked.

"Oh God, this is not happening," Mackenzie muttered.

"Mac?"

"I would be honored to take you out," the obviously Italian man told her in accented English.

"Oh. My. God. Is what I think is happening, really happening?" Jade laughed.

"It was seriously a joke. My friend and I-"

"Look, you're hot. I was already thinking it. You just said it first," he stated, cutting off her back peddling.

"No, no, no..."

"Do it, Mac!" Jade yelled.

"I'm Alfonzo," he introduced.

"Mackenzie," she said dryly.

"Then it's settled. I'll see you tonight at 7, Mackenzie." With no more than a smile and wink, he turned away and left her standing there gawking.

"What the hell just happened?" Mackenzie muttered, still standing in shock.

"You have a date!" Jade answered.

"It was a joke! That wasn't real! What the hell?!"

"It may have been a joke to you but not to him!" Jade exclaimed. Mackenzie could even imagine her bouncing all over her house.

"I'm not really going. He's not really going. Is he?! Am I?! What have you gotten me into?" Mackenzie rambled.

"Yes. Yes. Yes! You're going! Think of it as an experiment! You need to know!"

"I hate you right now," Mackenzie stated flatly.

"I love you, too. You're going!" Jade insisted.

"If I get stood up..."

"Then you can go home alone and happy after a nice meal," Jade interjected.

"Ugh..."

"Does this mean we are going shopping again?" Jade asked excitedly.

"No. Not happening. He can deal with what I already have."

The two talked more as Mackenzie started walking again. Jade kept pushing for Mackenzie to give this guy a real shot and Makenzie kept pushing back. She would never fully admit it to herself, much less to anyone else, but the thought of going out with anyone besides Nicolai made her stomach turn. She tried to shake it away, but it just wouldn't leave.

The topic finally turned to more mundane things and they settled into safer territory. Laughter on both sides filled the air and Mackenzie was back to getting strange looks from people she passed. Eventually, she reached the gym and stopped outside.

"Well, girl, I have to go," Mackenzie told her reluctantly.

"What do you have planned this morning?" Jade asked.

"I'm getting in the ring this morning. I need to beat the hell out of these nightmares, but a guy twice my size with have to suffice," Mackenzie told her.

"Boxing?"

"Kickboxing. You remember I always loved it growing up. It's kinda my thing now. What about you?"

"Just work, as usual. Have fun tonight! Eat well, if nothing else," Jade joked.

"Yeah, yeah. If he turns out to be some psycho, I'm holding you personally responsible," Mackenzie warned

The two said their good-byes and disconnected the call as Makenzie took a deep steadying breath before stepping inside. She looked around and found the biggest guy she could, sizing him up. As she walked up to him, she noticed he stood a full head and shoulders taller than her and had arms as big around as her waist.

"You'll do," she commented.

Hours later, her body was sore, but her mind was clear. The problem at hand, however, was the man walking towards her grinning like a loon. She was standing outside the agreed upon café at 6:58, willing herself not to just turn and run away. She had asked herself a million times why she was there, but couldn't for the life of her find an answer.

A devilish smirk and a perfectly kissable jawline sprang to mind and she had her answer. Jade was right. She needed to know if this was just because she was lonely, and had been for so long, or if she was actually hung up on someone she couldn't have. She steadied herself and plastered what she hoped was a friendly smile on her face.

"You showed up!" Alfonzo greeted as he reached her.

"Yep, I'm here," Mackenzie replied, trying to sound as cheery as he did.

"I didn't think you would," he chuckled.

"Me either," she admitted.

"Shall we?" he asked, ushering her inside before she could change her mind.

They were seated quickly at a table by the window and soon left alone in awkward silence. He smiled at her, but that's all it was. A smile. No butterflies. No pressure because of an underlying attraction. Just lead in her stomach and a smile.

"So, Bella, how are you this evening?" he finally asked, breaking the silence.

"I'm good. You?" she replied briefly, trying not to cringe at the endearment.

"I am wonderful! I am having dinner with the most beautiful woman in Sicily," he answered dramatically.

"Oh boy," Mackenzie mumbled, forcing a polite giggle. She looked away from the table to hide her exasperated expression and hoped he believed it was out of shyness instead.

"Have you been here before?" he questioned.

"Once or twice" Mackenzie answered truthfully. "They have a wonderful Pasta alla Norma."

"Your Italian is as beautiful as you are," he commented, drawing another inward cringe from Mackenzie.

"Would it be easier to switch to Italian for you?" she offered, trying to find some way to be nice.

"I wouldn't dream of it," he countered. "It is rare that I get to indulge in such an exotic accent with such a beauty."

"Really laying it on thick," she murmured under her breath.

"I'm sorry?" he asked, not catching what she said.

"Uh ...I said ...um ...can we dial the compliments back a bit?" She tried to find something else to say that sounded similar to her actual statement, but eventually hit him with the truth.

"Oh, you don't mean that!" Alfonzo retorted, losing none of his overly friendly tone. "You American women try so hard to play modest, but we know the truth."

"The truth?" She raised an eyebrow at him.

"Yes! You do that as a way to get even more compliments!"

"Oh no...no no...I-"

"Don't worry Bella, I have all the compliments you crave but are too shy to ask for," he said cheerfully.

"Oh goody..." she replied dryly.

Mackenzie picked up her menu and tried to look interested in it. In truth, she was trying to hide her traitorous facial expressions from the man that, probably, was a genuine lady's man across from her. He had probably been right, there were women who survived off of compliments. Not her, though. Too many seemed overboard and insincere, but even one made her uncomfortable.

She thought back to her date with Nicolai and how he had called her beautiful. Somehow, his compliment had left her breathless and tingly, not feeling cheap and gross like Alfonzo's. She had been nervous on that date, yes, but not out of not wanting to be there. Nicolai had taken care to calm her fears and still banter with her. His easy or mischievous smiles were in clear contrast to Alfonzo's presumably charming one that was plastered permanently to his face.

The only real similarities between the two men was the dark hair, and even then, they weren't the same shade. Nicolai was tall, Alfonzo was average. Green eyes vs brown. Beard vs clean shaven. Broad shoulders and muscled vs average build. Feisty and playful vs inorganically complimentary.

She shook her head and tried desperately to push those thoughts away. She reminded herself why she was there. Why she could never ever be with Nicolai. Why she couldn't be with anyone, ever. She looked up at Alfonzo and realized he had been talking to her all along and she hadn't been paying attention. She gave a soft smile and nodded her head, hoping she didn't just agree to something she would regret later.

The waiter arrived to take their orders and Mackenzie decided to push some buttons, pull a page from Nicolai's book. Anything to try to have more fun than watching paint dry.

"Do you trust me?" she playfully asked.

"What?" Alfonzo asked, confused.

"I said, do you trust me?" she repeated. "I'll order for both of us."

"Oh, don't you worry your pretty head. I've already handled it!" he replied eagerly.

The waiter took that has his cue to leave as quickly as possible.

"You what?" She didn't remember him speaking to the server, but she had admittedly been in her own thoughts.

"Yes, I assumed you don't eat much, being as small as you are, so I ordered you a side salad!" He was so proud of himself.

Mackenzie stared at him, slack jawed, in disbelief.

"Oh, don't worry. No thanks are necessary," he continued. "I need to step to the bathroom for a moment, but when I get back, I want to hear all about where you grew up."

Mackenzie was still in shock as he walked away. A side salad, really?! Where she grew up?! She placed her face in her hands and slumped her shoulders.

"Shoot me now."

Chapter 6

Nicolai watched Mackenzie in what seemed like the most awkward date ever from the other side of the café. The excitement of seeing her had given way to shock as she was seated with another man. Something that felt uncharacteristically like jealousy had almost knocked him out of his chair. She didn't owe him anything. In fact, she had told him more than once that she was not interested in him and his 'mafia ties'. So why did he still feel a claim on her?

He had learned in such a short time how to read her body language and his jealousy soon gave way to amusement. This guy was crashing faster than the Titanic and didn't even know it. For some unknown reason, Mackenzie seemed to be desperately trying to be nice to this guy and, in the process, was inching closer and closer to an explosion. The way she stayed hidden behind her menu was a hilarious sign this guy wasn't catching as he continued to prattle on.

Nicolai knew that, at some point, he was going to step in and rescue her, he just wasn't sure how far he was going to let it go. He saw the smile he had come to love ease its way onto her face and laughed to himself. This poor guy didn't know she was about to eat him alive. But then the waiter ran away, presumably something Mr. Clueless said, and her smile turned to shock. As the guy smiled in triumph and walked away, Mackenzie slumped in defeat.

"That's my cue," he stated to himself before raising his voice to the rest of the table. "I'll see you guys around. I have some...things to attend to."

The table sounded off with various salutations, but Nicolai wasn't paying attention. He was focused on the woman who had held his every waking thought hostage. She looked miserable and totally miffed. She was lost in thought as he approached and never saw him before he sat across from her.

"Hey there, beautiful," he greeted with a lazy drawl.

Mackenzie snapped her head up and stared at the man across from her. She blinked her eyes a couple of times, not daring to look away. Nicolai sat in the chair where Alfonzo had been. Had she thought of him so hard that she was now hallucinating? Or was he truly there? If he was really there, where did he come from?

"Did you miss me?" he smirked.

Butterflies took flight in her stomach and she knew the answer. It was Nicolai. Only Nicolai. Mackenzie snapped out of her daze and anger suddenly coursed through her. "Are you following me? Are you having me followed?"

"You want to stay with Casanova all night? That's' fine, I'll go," Nicolai replied, moving to stand up.

"No, wait!" Mackenzie exclaimed, her hand shooting out to grab his arm. "I'm sorry, please don't go."

He smiled as he sat down once more. "I was here with some friends when I noticed the disaster taking place over here. Thought I could help out."

"I didn't mean to jump to conclusions. I'm just a little on edge. I don't want to be here," she confessed.

"Want to get out of here?" His smile was wickedly sexy and tempting.

"Yes!...No...I can't..." She deflated on the spot.

"Why not?"

"I swore to my bestie I would go through with this. I was trying to forget y -um...someone, and all this was her idea," Mackenzie told him.

"Would it help to know he was part of another Mafia family?" he asked, leaning across the table.

"Oh my God, really?!" she squeaked, freaking out and digging her fingers into his arm.

"I don't know, but do you really want to take that chance?" His eyes shimmered with mischief.

"Oh...oh! You're right! Better safe than sorry!" she agreed, beaming at him. Her gaze finally fell to where her hand was on his arm. "Oh! I'm sorry!"

Nicolai grabbed her hand as she tried to pull away. He held it softly between both of his.

"Don't be," he told her softly. He lifted her hand to his lips and placed a chaste kiss on the back of it.

"I hate to be the non-gushy one here, but he's coming back any minute," Mackenzie reminded him.

Nicolai stood with a laugh and pulled her to her feet. He turned to leave the restaurant, pulling her behind him with the hand he still held. She never stopped to look back as they made their escape. For once, the fear of getting caught was more of a rush than an anxiety inducing death sentence. She couldn't hide the smile that forced its way onto her face.

She knew she shouldn't go with him, she should run the other direction, but something drew her to him. He was adventure and sex appeal rolled into one incredibly hot package. This was the most fun she had had in as long as she could remember, and they hadn't even made it outside yet. He glanced back at her in that exact moment and winked, as if he, too, felt the same way.

They burst onto the street and Nicolai never broke his stride. She had no problem keeping up, her long legs matching his step for step. Mackenzie searched the road for his sports car but couldn't find it. When he finally stopped, she asked him.

"Where is your car?"

"I brought the bike tonight," he replied devilishly.

Looking behind him, Mackenzie started shaking her head. "No way, can't do it," she told him.

"Why not?" he poked.

"I am in a skirt! A tight one!" she pointed out what she thought was obvious.

"I noticed. No little black dress for this guy. You look like you just came from work instead. Either way though, you're still incredible," he told her, confirming that he knew exactly what she was wearing.

"So, how am I supposed to ride a motorcycle?!"

"Hike it up. Let's go," he smirked. "Want me to close my eyes?"

"You're insane! Do you know how tight this thing is?!"

"Oh, trust me...I do," he replied, his eyes hooded with something more than mild appreciation.

Mackenzie flushed at his words, losing all steam. There was a hunger in his eyes as he looked her over from head to toe that took her breath away. Chills cascaded down her spine in anticipation of what the night might bring. He swung one leg over and straddled the seat, making her even more aware of the position they would be in.

"Do you trust me?" he chuckled, holding hand out to her.

"You need a new line," she teased, still not moving. Her mouth ran dry as images of what she wanted to do to him ran through her mind, conjured by the sexy way he positioned himself on the bike. "And I need a drink."

"The choice is yours, come with me, or stay here with lover boy," he stated, pointing behind her.

"Bella?!" Alfonzo called out from the doors, accentuating Nicolai's point.

"Fuck!" Mackenzie exclaimed as she started pulling her skirt up. "Thank God for spandex."

"Thank God, indeed," Nicolai agreed, laughing.

"If my skirt rips..." she warned.

"I will take full responsibility and buy you a new one," he promised, helping her climb on behind him. "Hold on tight."

Mackenzie, against her better judgement, molded her body to his and wrapped her arms around his waist. The bike roared to life, drowning out the shouts from Alfonzo. Nicolai pulled into the street and hit the gas, making her tighten her grip so she didn't fall off. Her laughter was all Alfonzo was left with as they sped away.

***

An hour later, Mackenzie and Nicolai walked along an empty stretch of beach. Her heels and his boots were left behind at the motorcycle and his jeans were rolled up slightly. The surf lapped at their feet and greasy street food filled their hands.

"A fucking salad! No, side salad! Not even an entire salad, only a part of one? Cheap ass! Do I look anorexic? I can probably out eat him any day of the week! Fucking side salad. That's insulting!" Mackenzie ranted in between bites.

Nicolai laughed so hard he was in serious danger of dropping his own meal. "I knew something had happened when the server ran for cover, but never did I think it would be this good!"

"Good? This isn't good! Side. Salad. There are not enough compliments in the world to make up for that. And trust me, he had already been doing that...all...night," she continued. "Oh Bella, you are so beautiful! American women fish constantly for compliments, but don't worry, you'll have all you'll ever want right here," she said in a mocking tone. "Fuck you!"

Her voice echoed off the waves around them. She paused her tirade and took another bite, chewing carefully.

"What would you have done if I hadn't come along?" he asked moments later.

"I don't know. I like to think I could have kept my cool, made it through, and gone home. After stopping to grab actual food, that is. But honestly, I probably would have ended up throwing my drink or food at him, or hell, punching him, then storming out," she confessed before shoving more food in her mouth.

"You wouldn't have let him..." He purposefully left the question open ended.

"Take me home? Kiss me? Have his way with me? Am I warm here?" she asked for clarification.

"Red hot," he admitted.

"Hell no. There is no scenario where that man will ever know where I live or even touch my hand," she promised.

Nicolai exhaled the breath he didn't know he had been holding. Relief rolled through his body.

"Then why were you out with him?"

"I...oh what the hell. It's not like I've held any punches with you so far anyway, might as well stick my whole foot in my mouth instead of just my toes. So, that day in the coffee shop, when we met, my best friend was on the phone...like...almost the entire time," she admitted.

"Seriously? I didn't see-"

"Blue tooth," she offered.

"Ah. Didn't think about that."

"Anyway, she's the reason I said yes, or rather, the reason I allowed myself to say yes. Then the whole Mafia thing...somehow you got in my head, and even with the undesirables, I couldn't shake it. Her cure, if you will, was to go on another date with someone...not you."

"And you did it? Those are some impressive powers of persuasion," he smirked.

"Well...I kinda...accidentally asked out some random guy on the street. Or, at least, that's how he took it." She watched as her toes dug into the soft sand as she walked rather than look at his reaction.

"Accidentally?"

"I was goofing around, barking out times and locations like a drill sergeant and he was like 'yes' before I could do anything else. I tried explaining it was all a joke, but he just ran off. By that point, my bestie was dying and demanded I show up simply for experiments sake. A comedy of errors led me here tonight, you could say," she finished.

"I have got to meet your best friend," Nicolai laughed.

"If only," Mackenzie mused sadly.

"So, this was all a way to forget about...me?" he questioned, missing her softly spoken words.

"Foot. In. Mouth," she commented. "Yep."

"And now?" He raised an eyebrow as he looked down at her.

"Now? Devil you know versus the Devil you don't?" she suggested, shrugging her shoulders as she stared into his eyes.

"What if I told you I'm not a bad guy. That what you see isn't all of what you get?" he asked, stopping their walk to look at one another. He needed to see her reaction, to see her relief.

"I'd say I know you crime family types. Don't promise me something you can't deliver," she whispered, years of pain making her words heavy.

"Okay, filing that away to examine later," he murmured. "I'm not with the Mafia, not in any way."

"What?" Confusion laced her voice. "Then why were you with them?"

"I'm under cover. I have been for years. It's finally almost over, though," he told her. "A few more people to round up and I'll be free of this."

"Why are you telling me this?" she asked, her mind spinning with all the new information. "Can't this get you killed?"

"It can," he agreed. "In the hands of the wrong person. But I couldn't stand to see the look in your eyes when you saw me as one of them. I'm not one of them and I never will be."

Mackenzie swayed on her feet and he wrapped his arms around her to keep her steady. A cop. An undercover cop. It all made sense. How he found her at the festival. How he got away from the raid. Why he felt the need to protect her from Lorenzo. He expected her to be thrilled by this, relieved, but it was still just as complicated as before for reasons she couldn't tell him. He wasn't the Mafia. He wasn't like her ex-husband. She clung to that thought and pushed the rest away to deal with later.

"Say something," he begged, watching a range of emotions roll across her face.

"So, I stole a cop's gun?" she questioned, a sassy smile on her face. "Is that anything like assault?"

"That was a gift, and one well used," he laughed, the tension broken. Even though he could tell she was scared, of what he didn't know, she was still as playful as ever.

"Hmmm...so no handcuffs then?"

"Not unless you beg," he replied, leaning down within an inch of her face.

She inhaled sharply at his nearness, catching a hint of his spicy yet earthy scent. The low rumble of his voice coursed through her body and shot straight to her core. Somehow, his bombshell had broken through the rest of her defenses, leaving her body free to openly respond to his flirtations

"You once told me, that if I ever kissed you again, you would shoot me," he reminded her breathlessly. "Does that still stand?"

Her eyes were drawn to his lips as her own tongue ran absentmindedly along her bottom lip. "Nope."

He didn't waste any time drawing her to him and pressing her lips to his. This time was soft and sweet, nothing like the all-consuming, claim making kiss of before, but just as mind numbingly amazing. The world fell away and took all the reasons this was a bad idea with it. His hands moved over her body slowly, as if memorizing every curve and coaxing her into letting go completely.

Her hand moved to his face and cupped his jaw as her mouth parted, inviting him in. The low growl emitted from his throat sent liquid heat pooling at her center. His tongue dove inside and claimed her, exploring every inch, tangling with hers as he pulled her closer to him.

The kiss quickly escalated from sweet to simmering and when they finally pulled apart, they were both breathing heavy and clinging to one another. Mackenzie knew she should move away, even as something familiar tugged at her, but she couldn't bring herself to do it. Instead, she stayed tangled in his arms.

"Let's get out of here," Nicolai mumbled breathlessly.

Mackenzie nodded her approval as he laced his fingers with hers. Together, they silently retraced their steps to where the bike was waiting and quickly climbed on. Nicolai didn't ask where they were going, he just steered the bike along an invisible path. One hand left the handlebars to lay across her arms, which were wrapped tightly around him.

The feel of her pressed so tightly against him was impairing his ability to concentrate. He swerved quickly as her lips began placing small, soft kisses along the base of his neck. He felt her smile against him as he moaned his approval of her actions. He was not prepared for what she would do next.

Mackenzie gave into the feelings she felt for Nicolai. She still wasn't sure that being a cop was better than a mobster in the grand scheme of her life at the moment, but she was done denying this connection between them. At least for tonight. Tonight, she wanted him closer than she had let anyone in years.

The moan that escaped him as she kissed his neck spurred her on. She felt bold and feisty as she swung under his arm and slid around his body, straddling his lap in between him and the handlebars in one swift motion. The shock on his face was priceless and she snuggled into his chest to hide the laughter in her eyes.

His scent, stronger now due to their nearness, teased her. He revved the engine and the force pressed her fully against his rock-hard body. She realized her mistake as her skirt slid even higher up her thighs, pressing her firmly against his bulging jeans. Her eyes flew to his in an instant. They were hooded and muddled with desire, which only seemed to boost her confidence and her libido.

Her eyes were drawn to his throat as he swallowed hard. Giving into temptation she kissed the hollow of his neck and shoulder, nipping and teasing as she relished in the soft growl that escaped him.

"Damn it, Mac. I swear if you don't stop, we're not going to make it to your place," Nicolai said, his voice low and husky. His arm wrapped around her back and held her close.

Her soft laugher brushed across his exposed skin and sent shivers through his body. He fought hard to concentrate on driving, on getting them safely to their destination. Just the feel of her body pressed against his was enough to drive him crazy, but the feel of her mouth against his neck and shoulder tested the limits of his control.

"My place?" she purred.

"I was going to take you to mine, but yours is closer," he admitted.

"Fair," she replied lightly, wrapping her legs tighter around his waist.

Nicolai gave a sigh of relief as he spotted her apartment with an empty space right by her door. He eased the bike into the space and killed the engine. As he stood, he slid his arms under her legs and took her with him, still wrapped around his waist.

"What about the neighbors?" Mackenzie laughed. "My skirt is practically at my waist!"

"Do you know your neighbors?" he asked gruffly.

"Well, no," she replied thoughtfully.

"Then it doesn't matter," he chuckled.

Mackenzie's giggles filled the air as they continued up the sidewalk to her door. Her feet finally touched the ground once they got there and she smoothed her skirt back into place. She searched for her keys as his lips kissed slowly along her shoulder.

"You aren't making this any easier," she joked, fumbling with her keys.

"And that stunt on my bike did?" he retorted. "But you better hurry up, or we are going to give your neighbors a real show."

Finally, the key worked and the door opened, dropping both of them inside with a fit of giggles. Nicolai kicked the door closed behind them and pulled her to him, not bothering to move from their position on the floor. He looked around briefly before returning his attention to her.

"Nice place you got here," he commented before kissing her neck again.

"Oh shut up, Niko," she groaned as his hand slid up her thigh.

His smile against her skin was tantalizing. The roughness of his beard in contrast to the smooth, softness of his lips made her body beg for more. Her hands clung to his broad shoulders as her back arched, pressing her breasts against his chest. As his fingers teased along the edges of her panties, she began pulling his shirt over his head.

Mackenzie gasped at the sight before her. She had seen him shirtless at the beach, but she had been actively avoiding looking at him. Now, though, she could drink it all in. Her fingers trailed over his firm, barreled chest and down his toned abs. She leaned up and ran her tongue over what she somehow knew would be a sensitive area between his pecs. His swift intake of breath rewarded her as her hands continued to roam.

Her fingers ran over a scar on his left side and her hand stilled. She all but quit breathing as her mind raced. She pushed him away slightly as she sought out the scar, needing to see it with her own eyes as panic began to well up inside of her. When she found it, running from halfway to his back to almost his belly button, her breath whooshed out of her.

"Is everything okay?" he asked, suddenly feeling self-conscious.

"This scar, where did you get it?" she asked in a whisper.

"I had a motorcycle accident in high school," he replied casually.

"Undercover...Niko isn't your real name, is it?" she questioned, trying to keep from dissolving into hysterics.

"No, it isn't. I'll tell you my real name when this is all over, but it could be dangerous to tell you now," he confessed.

Mackenzie rolled away from him, her mind trying desperately to come to terms with everything she had learned. She was careful not to run her hands through her hair as per her usual response to her world seemingly falling apart around her.

Nicolai sat up slowly and replaced his shirt. He wasn't used to that scar causing such an unusual response and it seriously confused him. He studied her face and body posture, recognizing all the signs of PTSD which only surprised him more. She looked up at him and blinked slowly. A flash of green caught his attention and he paused.

"Are you wearing colored contacts?" he asked, something telling him it was important.

Mackenzie's eyes grew wide at his question. Her breathing shallowed and not in a good way. "I think you should leave."

"What?" That wasn't the response he was expecting.

"Please leave." Mackenzie wrapped her arms around her waist to keep from reaching for him as they both stood.

Nicolai reached out a hand and wiped away the tear that escaped her eyes. "I'll call you. I don't know what this is, but I'll find out. And then, I'll call you."

He turned and walked out the door, closing it safely behind him. She slid to the floor, unable to stand any longer as the tears began to flow.

"Jaxon Haier, what the hell are you doing here?"

Chapter 7

Jaxon sat in the office of the house he was using while undercover, staring at the computer screen. His mind was a blur, sorting through everything that had happened that night. Seeing Mackenzie on a date with someone else had been a definite blow but knowing it was because of her attraction to Nicolai? To him? It was a light in the darkness that his life had become.

Rescuing her from Mr. Compliments was invigorating and the ride through the city with her at his back was fun. He remembered their walk on the beach and her outrage over the side salad making a hearty laugh escape him in the empty room. Then that kiss, that kiss had rocked his world and left him wanting more. The motorcycle acrobatics proved that she had felt the same.

As much as he wanted to remember the beginning of their time in her apartment, it was really how it ended that intrigued him. His scar had elicited some interesting reactions before, but PTSD episodes were not one he was accustomed to. The colored contacts threw him for a loop as well. He knew he had been lying about who he was, but it never occurred to him that she could be doing the same.

It made sense, though. She said she wanted to leave the past in the past on their first date and she had been so nervous, so unlikely to trust. He remembered her eyes darting around, mapping out escape routes. The way she handled a gun, his gun, when she found out he was 'mafia' was classic 'I won't be a victim again' mentality. Come to think of it, she didn't seem all that relieved when he told her he was a cop. If she was on the run from someone, a cop could be just as dangerous as a criminal when you're trying to blend in and lay low.

Then there was the scar incident. Could it have reminded her of whomever had caused her PTSD? Was it a cop with a scar? Mobster maybe? Did he look like her attacker? Sound alike? Had it been sexual in nature? He had to know what it was, but he doubted she would just tell him, especially after everything she knew about him.

Pulling up the screen in front of him, he logged into the police database. He typed what he knew about her into the search and sat back. Southern USA. Brown hair. 5'6". Freckles. Blue or green eyes. Mackenzie. Eventually, a couple hits came back, but nothing that matched her or a situation able to leave permanent damage.

It was a dead end. He sat back in his chair, his elbows rested on the arms of the chair and his fingers steepled in front of his chest. There had to be something he was missing. He reexamined every time they had met, every conversation, every change in posture, any trigger.

"That's it," he murmured to himself in the silence.

The dream. The name. Jaxon. If she could change her eye color, she could change her hair color, too. Something had drawn him to her from the very start, something like a memory that wouldn't quite focus. He hadn't seen it, hadn't put the pieces together for one very good reason. She was dead.

But what if she wasn't? What if she had faked her death and ran? At the time, he had been so devastated by the news that he hadn't wanted to know how she had died, but now, he needed to know everything. He typed her name into the search bar. Fiona Lancaster.

Her face instantly popped up on screen. Her green eyes and copper hair had the same mesmerizing, combination he remembered them to be. He studied her face and thought about Mackenzie. Makenzie was older, but not in a bad way. There was a definite difference in the eyes. Fiona looked so full of life and hope. Mackenzie looked like she had seen the worst humanity had to offer and made it through the other side, stronger but damaged.

Essentially, though, they could be the same woman. He clicked the button by her date of death and scenes from a car wreck filled the screen. As horrific as they were, they were pretty textbook for that kind of crash. Nothing seemed too out of the ordinary. Tractor trailer hit her car, sending both up in flames. Only way to identify the body was a driver's license in her right back pocket.

"Wait...that's not right," he mumbled, leaning in closer. "People change, but not that much."

Fiona always carried a small wallet in her back-left pocket if she wasn't carrying a purse. She hated carrying purses, but used them when she didn't have pockets to do the job. But it was ALWAYS her left pocket, the right was for her phone. Something was wrong.

Another name caught his attention. Fiona Walker. She had been married. He didn't know, but then again, he hadn't wanted to know. He clicked on that name and a large red box popped up stating 'restricted'.

"Now we're getting somewhere," he commented.

He reached for his cell and punched in Bertotti's number. They had worked together for years now and he trusted him to be discrete.

"Haier," Bertotti greeted as the line answered.

"I need a favor."

***

Jaxon. Jaxon Haier. The name ran through Mackenzie's head as she numbly trudged to work. It's no wonder she had been drawn to Nicolai so completely. Her soul recognized his even if her eyes didn't recognize his face. It wasn't totally surprising that she didn't know right away. They had just been kids, and he had been the love of her life.

They had been best friends since childhood and eventually started dating in high school. He was a star baseball player while she was in color guard in the marching band and they had been the quintessential couple. Everyone knew they would be married one day. When he had wrecked his bike, she had nursed him back to health. When she had torn her knee, he had stayed by her side. Their love had been unconditional and perfect.

Until the day he left.

They had just graduated, the summer was theirs to command before they went off to college together. They had planned to meet up and go hiking the Silver Comet Trail, but he never showed. His phone was shut off, never to turn on again. She was left behind, waiting, wanting, and completely discarded. Heartbroken and lost, she had searched for him, but he and his parents had vanished completely, not a trace to be found.

She had never been the same. Jade had convinced her to move on, and she did, sort of, but it was never the same. Jaxon Haier always had a huge chunk of her heart that he never gave back. If she was being entirely honest with herself, he had all of her heart.

That's why she was still in a state of shock as she walked to work. What was he doing here? What had led him to working undercover? Where the hell had he been all this time? Why had he left and why hadn't he said good-bye? Why did he have to show up now, after all this time, when everything was so broken?

Jade had been just as shocked to hear what she had learned that morning. Mackenzie thought it would be safer to have that conversation before leaving the apartment as there were too many potential ears on the street and she didn't need him getting killed because of her. Her bestie, once she got over the initial shock, had been quick to point out Mackenzie's dream and how she had called out Jaxon's name instead of Nicolai. Apparently, even her subconscious knew all along.

Jade, for all of her 'treat thy self' advice knew that this was dangerous for both of them. He was a cop, he was obligated to uphold the law. She was technically on the run after faking her death. He was probably already onto her after realizing she wore fake contacts. If he knew who she was, he would be forced to choose between his duty to the badge and the woman he once loved.

Mackenzie stopped at the thought. Once loved. Could he still love her? Would he still love her after everything that happened? Did she still love him?

She rolled her eyes at herself and resumed walking. Of course, she still loved him. She had already admitted that much to herself and to Jade. That was the problem. She loved him, but she was going to be the one to leave this time. And there was her answer. He couldn't know who she really was. This would kill her, but she loved him too much to drag him with her, to hurt him like he had hurt her all those years ago.

Mackenzie pulled out of her thoughts long enough to realize she was at work. She needed to focus on something, anything, other than Jaxon tonight. She would figure out later if she would ever see him again or if it was time for a change of scenery already. She didn't want to leave yet. Maybe he would be reassigned out of the area. She knew it was all wishful thinking, but it didn't matter.

She went directly to the employee lounge once inside the building and began putting her things away. She stopped to look in the mirror and brush a rogue hair back in place. She took a deep breath as she pushed all thoughts out and stepped onto the floor, smile plastered to her face.

The evening was smooth enough, no issues with tables, no Mafia looming over her, no Nicolai/Jaxon. Makenzie avoided any talk about Nicolai from Elise as she was sure to mess up and say the wrong thing. Instead, she mainly nodded and agreed with whatever was being said and continued on her way.

As the crowd started to slow, she found that she had no way to avoid her bosses prying eyes. Mackenzie tried to busy herself by cleaning tables and chairs, but the Italian woman just wasn't having it. She planted herself firmly in Mackenzie's path and refused to budge.

"Do you mind? I'm trying to work here," Mackenzie huffed, trying to sound put out instead of nervous.

"Nu-uh, you don't get away that easy," Elise stated, cornering her. "You've been quiet all night. What's going on here?"

"I don't know what you're talking about. I'm just trying to do my job," Mackenzie hedged.

"You think I don't see you looking over your shoulder all night? Is it Niko? The Mafia? Are you hoping to see them or not?" Elise's hands were on her hips now.

"It's complicated," Mackenzie placated, moving to another table.

"Complicated. Story of my life," Elise chuckled. "You know what you need? A night out!"

"Oh no! That's what got me into this mess!" Mackenzie reminded, shaking her head.

"I mean a girls night! No men involved!"

"I mean...okay! Sounds good!" Mackenzie was surprised at Elise's offer. Sure, they were friends, but that generally extended to work and the occasional bite to eat. "When?"

"Now! The lounge is slow, they can handle any last-minute people. Put yourself back together and let's go!"

"Wait! Where are we going?" Mackenzie called out as Elise walked away.

"Teatro Messimo Bellini! There is a concert there tonight I want to see. It's near Villa Bellini so if it sucks, we could go chill and catch up on our oxygen intake," Elise joked.

"Very funny," Mackenzie replied dryly. "I don't just hide out in my apartment. I do actually go outside, you know."

"Either way, let's go."

The two of them hurried to the employee area and gathered their things. It wasn't long before they were out of the club and hailing a taxi. The drive to the venue was filled with traffic, but they didn't mind. They joked and gossiped together like old friends while Mackenzie was carefully steering the conversation away from her and Nicolai.

Teatro Massimo Bellini was a massive building that housed everything from Operas and plays to grand events and concerts. Tonight's concert was by a band who touted their style as a little rock, a little classical, and a whole lot of heart. Mackenzie had never heard of them and had no idea what that was supposed to mean, but she was up to the challenge. She was thankful Elise had dragged her out, it was something Jade would approve of.

The taxi pulled up in front of the imposing venue and the two of them got out.

"Um...we are not dressed for this," Mackenzie stated, finally remembering their work clothes.

"Don't worry, this band attracts a ton of diverse groups of people. We won't stand out any more than that guy," Elise promised, pointing to a man wearing a green, strappy body suit with matching spiked mohawk.

"Yikes!" Mackenzie replied, watching him enter the venue. "Fair enough."

The concert was general admission, so they bought their tickets from the box office and went inside to find a good place to watch from.

"Let's get drinks!" Elise proclaimed excitedly, pumping her fists into the air.

"Oh no...I'm good. I prefer to drink alone in the safety of my own house," Mackenzie protested, shaking her head and holding her hands out.

"Water then?" Elise asked.

"Sounds great!"

Elise trudged away through the growing crowds, leaving Mackenzie alone to look around. They had found their way pretty close to the stage, which was huge with an elaborate set up for the band. Along the sides of the room were private boxes, the kind she had seen in movies about operas. Turning her attention to the people around her, she thought of the differences between here and the US.

The people around her really were from all walks of life. Some looked like bankers, others looked like urchins from the seediest underworld and everything in between. They all gathered for a cause, none of them offended by the existence of the other. Acceptance and unity were at its most basic. The crowd, as a whole, gave off a vibe unlike any other she had been around.

"You better hurry, Elise," she commented to herself as the room got more and more crowded. She began to worry her friend would be unable to find her.

Finally, all 5'2" of spunk came barreling through the people around her to reach Mackenzie with a beer in one hand and a water in the other.

"Sorry, had to flag someone down. Apparently, I'm short," Elise grumbled.

"Really? I hadn't noticed," Mackenzie joked looking over her head

"Shut up and take your water before you wear it," Elise commented, her eyes wide as she stared her down.

The lights dimmed as Mackenzie took her drink. The band took the stage as the audience erupted into cheers, including Elise. Mackenzie laughed to herself but played along, wooing for the band. The introduction was short and sweet, and soon music filled the room.

While Elise sang along, Mackenzie swayed with the music, not knowing a single song but not disliking her time. Eventually, Mackenzie picked up part of a chorus here or there and joined in, enjoying herself. The energy of the room was infectious and before long it didn't matter that she didn't know the lyrics. Everyone was one large, happy family, united by music.

Someone bumped into Mackenzie a few songs in, apologizing immediately. She assured them there was no issue and returned her attention to the stage. When it happened again a few minutes later, she turned back, expecting to see the same enamored man. Instead, she found two large, imposing men in suits with the obvious bulge of guns under their jackets.

"You need to come with us" one of them told her. His voice was cold, leaving no room for argument.

"What's this about?" Mackenzie questioned, stalling for time to find an exit strategy.

"Our boss wants to speak to you," the other man added.

Mackenzie's eyes slid to Elise who seemed ready to cause a scene. She gave her friend a barely noticeable head shake, hoping Elise would be smart enough to stay out of it.

"It seems I'm being pulled away. Sorry to leave you like this. I'll see you later," Mackenzie shouted above the music, trying to give her the hint to leave once she and her escorts were gone.

"Okay, see you later!" Elise replied, getting the message loud and clear.

Mackenzie turned back to her armed escorts and motioned for them to lead the way. Her heart and mind raced with possibilities. She knew they were part of the Mafia without them saying anything. They were different from those at the club, though. Quiet. Serious. Higher up in rank, she was sure. These were the men who worked closely with the big boss. She knew this could all go sideways really quick if she didn't keep her wits about her.

They led her out of the main concert hall and up a winding staircase and, at the end of a long hallway, stopped outside of a closed door. Their knock was deafening in the quiet surrounding them. It didn't take long for the door to open, two more muscled men standing on the other side. Seeing who had knocked, they stepped aside for them to enter. One of the men with Mackenzie nudged her forward.

As they entered the room, Makenzie realized they were in one of the private suites overlooking the concert. Music drifted along from further in, breaking the silence that had followed them. The room looked normal enough, aside from the looming men leering at her. She squared her shoulders and stared at the obviously in charge man, refusing to cower or back down.

"That's her alright, I'd remember that ass anywhere," the man she remembered to be Lorenzo stated as he moved towards her.

"Mac, is it? Please, have a seat," the one in charge stated, motioning for a chair.

"It's Mackenzie, thanks. And I'll stand," she replied, making it known that she wouldn't be tested. She eyed the men around the room coolly, keeping her stance calm and relaxed, even as she stopped at Lorenzo.

"I don't care for women who don't do as I say," he sneered, his eyes narrowing at her.

"And I don't care for men who drag me away from my friends while I'm having a good time. So say what you want to say or

I'm out." She stood her ground and crossed her arms over her chest as her gaze returned to the man in charge. Her eyes bore into his and she quirked an eyebrow at him.

"Check her for weapons, she likes guns," Lorenzo laughed.

"Don't you dare," she warned, glaring at anyone near her.

"I've heard stories about you. Well, one in particular, in a club you work at." The Don's tone was accusatory as he watched her.

"Then you should know, if I pull a gun, I am fully prepared to use it," she informed him.

"You don't seem to have a gun on you now," he smirked.

"I didn't then either, and we aren't exactly in public this time," Mackenzie reminded them. "So again I say, tell me why I'm here or I'm out."

"We know about your 'boy toy', as you American's say," he began, smiling.

"Boy toy? I don't know who you're talking about," she replied, giving a carefully staged confused expression.

"Niko," Lorenzo offered.

"He's not my-"

"Oh, don't play dumb with me. That stunt with the gun was enough to fool some people, but not me," the Mafia boss cut her off harshly. The smile returned to his face before he continued. "We know he's with the police. He had me fooled for a while, but I've learned things recently. When you see him again, warn him."

"First off, that's news to me!" she exclaimed, years of hiding her true reactions behind calculated ones coming to her aid. "And second, why would you tell me this?"

"If you truly don't know he's a cop, then maybe this needs to be a warning to you too, as it seems you aren't who you say you are either." He paused and looked at her knowingly but did not elaborate. "But beyond that, I'm not an unreasonable person. He seems like a nice guy and I want him to know my men are coming for him. I don't like to kill unsuspecting cops."

"That's strangely...decent of you," Mackenzie replied warily. "Anyway, nice chatting with you. If that's all, I should probably be going now. My friend will be looking for me."

"She already left," one of the other men announced.

"Oh, well, then I should be leaving, too. Long day tomorrow." Relief that Elise had left flooded through her, but now she had to find another way to leave.

"Maybe she should stay with us," Lorenzo suggested.

"How can she deliver my warning if she's with us?" the man in charge sneered. "No, no. That won't do. You are free to go."

"Just like that?" she asked, trying to feel for a trap.

"Just like that," he confirmed.

"Then have a good night gentlemen," Mackenzie stated as she moved towards the door

The two guarding the door never moved as she approached. Mackenzie eyed them both, mentally sizing them up and planning her attack if they refused to let her leave. Carefully, she looked over her shoulder, raising an eyebrow in question.

"One more thing," he called out. "I may not know who you are yet, but rest assured, I will find out. And we will meet again."

"Lovely," she replied sarcastically.

She turned back to the door to find the men had finally opened it and she was free to leave. She walked confidently through the door and down the hall, refusing to give them the satisfaction of seeing her run. She held her composure down the stairs and to the main entrance. Once outside, however, she broke into a sprint as the rain began to fall from the sky.

She looked around wildly, searching for a taxi. She wanted to get as far away as possible before they changed their mind. Thoughts of calling Jaxon ran through her mind, but she quickly dismissed them. That's what they wanted. They were using her to get to him. She couldn't let that happen.

Even as she was being drenched by the pouring rain, she felt the presence of someone following her. Glancing over her shoulder discretely, she saw Lorenzo at the entrance to the theater. She had to find a taxi and fast. She couldn't let him follow her.

The light of a taxi pierced the rain and was headed straight for her. Her arm flew into the sky to hail it, but someone else got to it first. Frustrated, she looked around again but couldn't find another one. She thought about just walking home, but that wasn't really an option with Lorenzo following her.

Just as she was about to turn and confront her shadow, a familiar voice called out through the rain.

"Mac! Get in!"

Chapter 8

Mackenzie swiveled in her seat, watching the traffic behind them as Nicolai bounced in and out of traffic. He had shown up just as Lorenzo was racing down the stairs, confirming her suspicions. Now, she was watching to be sure she wasn't still being followed. Nicolai, also, made sure they didn't have a tail.

"I think we're good," he finally stated, his eyes still on the rearview mirror.

"You make a pretty good getaway driver," she said appreciatively.

His chuckle was deep and warmed her rain-soaked body. "I used to do some racing back in high school."

Mackenzie's heart squeezed at the mention of his past. A past she remembered. A past she had been a part of. "Good thing," she replied carefully.

"Care to tell me what happened back there?" Nicolai asked, eyeing her in the glow of the dashboard.

"How about we start with how you knew I needed a quick getaway and where to find me?" she countered, curiosity outweighing the warning burned into her memory.

"Elise. She called as soon as you were out of sight. I told her to get out of there and that I'd make sure you were safe," he explained easily.

"Good thinking, Elise. Except, that's what they wanted."

"Come again?"

"You. It was about you. They know you are a cop. Lorenzo recognized me in the crowd and the guy at the top wanted me to warn you, but I'm pretty sure they were trying to draw you out and it freaking worked," she told him, aggravated she had put him in danger.

"Can't say I didn't see this coming. Lorenzo had a front row seat to our performance in the lounge," he commented after a few minutes. "But either way, I wouldn't have left you to them. I hope you know that." His green eyes looked back to her before returning to the road.

"I'm resourceful, I can manage," Mackenzie responded, huffing slightly at his comment.

"I know. That was never a question. I'm just saying that you're not alone."

Mackenzie turned to look out the window at the rain that continued to fall. Pain and loneliness sliced through her as his words echoed within her. If he knew the truth, would he still say those things? Not knowing why he left, how could she be sure he would still be on her side?

"What else did they say?" he asked knowingly.

"Why do you think they said more?" she dodged, refusing to look back at him.

"Because you don't scare easily. And you were scared."

Mackenzie shrugged her shoulders and shook her head. Finally, she turned back to him. "It was nothing."

Stopped at a traffic light, Nicolai studied her face for a long moment. "Fine, don't tell me. You don't have to. Just know that I'm here if you want to talk."

Her mouth remained clamped shut. To tell him the rest of the conversation would mean telling him she, at the very least, wasn't Mackenzie. At the worst...she refused to think about it. Instead she just watched out the front window, trying to forget a past that could never be.

Nicolai watched her out of the corner of his eye as he drove them to one of his many safe houses. He could guess what they had said to her, but it would only be a guess. For as strong as she was, something had spooked her pretty good. He wanted to pull her into him and hold her close, to tell her it would all be okay, but he couldn't. He knew she wouldn't be open to that kind of response at the moment. Besides, he was driving. So, he settled for reaching over and grasping her hand, squeezing it reassuringly.

"Where are we going?" Mackenzie finally asked, not recognizing the area.

"My place. Well, one of them," he answered. Seeing her worried expression, he continued. "Don't worry, they don't know about this one."

"I'm not sure this is a good idea," she began. "Maybe you should just drop me at home."

"Is that really what you want?" Nicolai asked, his voice low as if holding back some hidden emotion.

Mackenzie bit her bottom lip, the only outward sign of the inward struggle she was fighting. She didn't want to go home. She wanted to spend every moment possible with her lost love before she had to give him up once more. She wanted to wrap herself in his arms and forget the world existed. Those were the things she wanted, but she *needed* to get away. Being around him was much harder than she thought it would be, not telling him the truth.

She watched him carefully. The sound of rain on the roof of the car was the only sound louder than her own pounding heart. "No." The word tumbled out of her mouth before she could stop it, but it was the truth.

"You'll be safer with me," Nicolai told her, trying to calm her unspoken fears.

"I know." It was a half-truth. She would be safer from the Mafia, yes, but her heart was another story.

"Besides, we're already here."

The car pulled up to a huge villa, complete with privacy fence and iron gates. Mackenzie looked around in awe at the beauty, even through the downpour around them. Nicolai smiled at her unbridled appreciation as they drove through the gates.

"This place is incredible! You live here?" she asked.

"Here, and a couple others. Perks of being undercover. Free housing," he chuckled.

"I mean, there has to be an upside to having to associate with scum," she agreed. "You do have a garage, right? If not, we're about to get soaked."

"Again, you mean?" he joked, looking at her clothes.

"Yeah, sorry about your car," she replied sheepishly.

"Don't be. It was seized as well. It's not even mine."

"Oh, well good."

"And yes, there is an attached garage."

As if to prove his words, a garage door began opening and he pulled the car into the open bay and out of the rain. Stepping out of the car, Mackenzie realized how soaked she still was as her shoe sloshed water all over the concrete flooring.

"Great. Maybe I should have gone home after all," she muttered.

"Nonsense. We'll get you dried off. Don't worry." He took her hand and led her into the main part of the house, stopping in the kitchen. Leaving her there, he went in search of some towels.

Mackenzie looked around at the spotless kitchen. Whomever had lived there had expensive taste. The appliances were all top of the line and the cabinets clearly custom made. She slid off her shoes and placed her bare feet on the obviously expensive tile. She had wanted a place like this at one time. Warm. Inviting.

Nicolai returned with towels and a pair of sleep pants and his shirt. Mackenzie closed her eyes as the second part of her dream tried to surface. She pushed down the vision of Jaxon Haier loving her unconditionally, trying desperately to hide her thoughts from him.

"I have to make some phone calls. Them grabbing you tonight puts things into motion and I have to check in," he said, placing the items on the counter.

"Wait," she called out as he turned to leave. "Can't you wait till morning?"

"Why?" Nicolai turned to her, his eyes guarded.

"Can't you just...stay with me?" Mackenzie kicked herself for sounding so needy, but if she was being honest with herself, she did need him.

"Are you okay?" The concern in his voice jumped when he realized she was shaking. He pulled her into his arms. "You're freezing!"

Without thinking, he grabbed a towel and wrapped it around her. Methodically, he started drying her off, trying to get her warm and keep her from getting sick. He didn't realize the intimacy of the act until he was bent at her feet and his eyes caught a glimpse up her skirt. Embarrassment and lust mingled together as his eyes met hers.

"I think I got a little carried away," he said softly as he rose to his feet once more.

"A little?" she teased, raising an eyebrow.

"Your clothes are drenched. I should let you change." His voice was deep as his fingers fiddled with the zipper of her skirt, his actions in direct conflict with his words.

"Or, you could just lower that zipper," she replied softly.

His slow, easy smile sent her heart into overdrive. She hadn't meant to say the words out loud, but now that she had, she knew she meant them.

The zipper slowly lowered and her skirt fell to the floor, her cheeky lacy panties left on display. His breath hitched and heat flared in her cheeks. His hands skimmed her barely clothed derriere, sending longing through both of them. His eyes returned to hers in question, afraid of breaking whatever spell this was, afraid of scaring her away again.

Her eyes stayed trained on his as she removed her shirt, leaving her camisole behind. She stilled his hands when he reached for the bottom of the remaining garment. Questions ran through his mind.

"This one stays," she told him.

"But…it's soaked through," he reminded her.

"This one stays, and your hands remain on the outside of it. Those are the rules." Her tone was low but firm. She wanted him, but she would stop everything if he couldn't comply.

"Okay," he eventually agreed, seeing the finality in her words across her face.

His reward was her lips pressed against his as her hands tugged at his shirt. He laughed against her lips before tearing himself away to remove the offending garment, only to immediately pull her back to him.

"Pants," she reminded him between frenzied kisses.

"Upstairs first," he answered, picking her up and throwing her over his shoulder.

Her giggles mixed with his deep laughter as he hurried through the house and up the stairs, refusing to put her down. Her feet kicked playfully as she tried to wiggle her way down. His free hand snaked around and slapped the exposed skin of her ass which was close to his face. The sting of pain sent liquid heat pooling to her core, transforming her giggles into a moan.

"Behave or I'll do it again," he commented, his voice husky and deep.

"Promise?" she breathed, more turned on than she thought possible.

His response was more of a growl as he reached the end of the hall and pushed open the door to the master bedroom.

After practically tossing her to the center of the king-sized bed, he began removing his belt and jeans. Mackenzie quickly regained her senses and crawled towards the edge of the bed and Nicolai.

Her lips found his chiseled abs, trailing kisses along his impossibly warm skin as her hands worked to help him with his zipper. His breath hissed out through clenched teeth as her tongue traced a path along the creases in his 6-pack.

"Not fair," he growled, pulling her up to where they were eye to eye.

"Rules are rules," she replied playfully, circling his neck with her arms.

"Rules are meant to be broken," he chided, starting to lift her shirt.

"Not this one," she demanded pushing his hands down and moving off the bed. It was too late, the damage was done. Panic rose within her and her breathing labored as she moved across the room.

Her hands began to shake as images raced through her head. She squeezed her eyes shut, trying to focus on anything other than the anxiety welling inside her.

Calloused hands gently grabbed her shoulders as Nicolai walked carefully up behind her. Instead of fueling the panic within her, it slowly brought everything back into focus. He didn't say a word, just lent his strength as she fought to remain in control. As her breathing slowed, he slowly wrapped his arms around her, enveloping her more and more in his calm embrace.

Eventually, Mackenzie turned and buried her face in his chest, breathing in his scent while still hiding her eyes. She took deep, calming breaths as he held her close, running a hand softly over her hair and planting light kisses on the top of her head. Together, they stood there, entwined with one another as Mackenzie brought herself out of the past and back to the present, clinging to the only person to ever calm the storm.

"I'm so sorry," she whispered, finally finding the ability to speak.

"Shhh...don't be. We can stop if we need to," Nicolai replied reassuringly.

"No, I don't want to. It's just been...well...let's just say it's been a long time. I just need some control, some boundaries. My shirt staying on is that boundary I need. I'm sorry." She refused to look up at him, afraid of the judgement or disappointment in his eyes.

"I can do that. If you're sure this is what you want, I can respect your boundary," he promised sweetly. He guided her face to look at him. "You're safe here...with me. At any time, you say the word, no matter what or when, and it all stops."

All she could muster for a reply was a nod as her eyes landed on his lips. Slowly, she raised up on her toes and pressed her lips to his. It was slow and sweet as Nicolai allowed her to set the pace. Her hands moved their way over his chest and up to his shoulders as his hands held on to her hips. His grip tightened as she wove her fingers into his hair, pulling him down to deepen the kiss.

It didn't take long before the tone shifted into something much more. Soft and sweet took a back seat to the passion that resurfaced as their bodies pressed against one another. The rough texture of Nicolai's jeans rubbed against her bare legs, making her squirm as his tongue tangled with hers. His hands skimmed down her hips to cup the underside of her ample rear eliciting a moan of appreciation from them both. His mouth never left hers as he lifted her easily from the ground. Mackenzie's legs naturally wrapped around his waist, pressing her aching center against his rock-hard abs, separated only by the thin lacy fabric of her cheekies.

The feel of his heat against hers caused her back to arch, breaking their kiss and tossing her head backwards. His mouth trailed down her neck, leaving a line of kisses and chills behind. Nearing the bed, he tossed her back into the center before shedding his jeans and boxer briefs.

Her eyes roved hungrily over his body in all of his breathtaking nakedness. Every inch of him was muscled and etched in stone. Before she had her fill, however, he was moving towards her, stalking her as he crawled across the bed with a determined glint in his eyes. He covered her body with his, his erection pressing against her soft folds as his hand slid under her back.

With a twist of his fingers through the thin fabric, her bra was unhooked. Her eyes flew to his as confusion filled her being.

"You said the shirt had to stay, not the bra. I want it gone," he told her gruffly.

"Fair enough," she giggled, complying with his demand and impressed he had found a loophole she could live with.

As she discarded the unwanted object, his eyes scorched her body as if he could see through the cami. She held her breath for his reaction, trying to remember just how thin the fabric was.

"You're so beautiful," he breathed, lowering his face to her barely clothed chest.

Even through the fabric, she could feel the heat from his breath and it sent shivers through her body. Her nipples hardened in anticipation, unsure of what was to come. His mouth kissed along the edge of her top before dipping down to take the pebbled peaks into his mouth while his hand found the sensitive area between her thighs. Light flashed behind her eyes as she groaned and pressed herself further into his touch. She had to fight the urge to remove the obtrusive garment as his tongue worked its magic through the obstacle.

As his hand skimmed the edge of her cheekies, and his fingers gently probed the skin beneath, Mackenzie moaned and went in search of her own handful of fun. His breath caught as her hand wrapped around his manhood, bringing a smile to her face as she moved slowly over the hard shaft.

"Mac, that's playing with fire," he groaned, moving his face to bury into her neck.

"That's what I want," she replied breathlessly.

"You said you need boundaries, need control. I'm trying my damndest to respect that," he reiterated, his jaw clamped tight as she continued her deliciously slow movements.

"The only boundary is to stay on top of the shirt. You've found a way to work with that."

"Yes, but-"

"But nothing. I'm not a China doll and I don't want to be treated as one. Stop holding back," she insisted, tightening her grip slightly to make her point.

"In that case..." He shifted slightly and removed her panties, quickly retuning to slip one finger, then another into her wet heat.

Once again, their moans matched one another and he laid his forehead against hers.

"Damn, you're ready for me," he whispered.

"Niko," she cried out. Her hand was still firmly on his own desire as she tried desperately to guide him to where she needed him. "Please."

"Oh, begging will get you everything," he promised as he poised himself over her entrance.

Still he hesitated, his head lifting to look deep into her eyes. An unspoken question hung in the air between them. Even now, with his own desire so evident against her, he was giving her the chance to walk away. She shifted her hips in response, pressing him more firmly against her. It was all the answer he needed.

Instantly, he was inside her, filling her, stretching her like never before. Heat built inside her and her toes began to tingle as he slowly extracted himself, only to plunge even deeper. Every nerve ending was alive with sensation as her hips bucked, trying to match his rhythm. Her nails trailed down his shoulders and back, digging in.

"You're going to make me come," he stated, his breathing ragged.

"That's the point," she reminded him playfully.

"Well in that case..." He pulled out of her long enough to flip her to her stomach and to pull her up on her knees.

A satisfying smack filled the air as his hand bounced off her bare behind, followed by her groan of pleasure and surprise. He grabbed a handful of her hair and tugged her head back, earning another moan as he bent to her ear.

"You still like it rough?" he asked, his breath teasing her ear.

"God, yes," she hissed, her eyelids fluttering closed.

"Good."

His manhood slid easily back into her slick folds, going even deeper than before. The feel of her was intoxicating and all-encompassing, but the sight of her round ass bouncing as he slammed into her over and over was going to send him over the edge quickly. He reached for her hand and guided it down, silently imploring her to touch herself. He didn't want to go without her, but he knew he couldn't last long at that rate.

Her whimpers nearly undid him as he felt her tighten around him. He pulled her hair again, causing her back to arch as he drove into her faster and harder, pushing them both closer to the edge of climax. Their combined voices filled the room as they were unable to keep their pleasure contained. Nicolai fought to ensure Mackenzie climaxed before him, shattering into a million pieces seconds behind her.

Spent and exhausted, he slumped over her still air bound hips. He wrapped his arms around her, holding her tight as their breaths slowly began to return to normal. Mackenzie was lost to the sensations radiating through her body. Her heart raced even as her breathing slowed. The comfort of his arms around her brought her back to the world around them as his beating heart began to calm her own.

Begrudgingly Nicolai sat back up, using her hips as a brace. Slowly, he inched himself out of her, instantly feeling the loss of their connection. Mackenzie sighed as he began to back away, missing the feel of his solid strength. His hand slid from her hip and a curious sound reached her ears as his weight shifted off the bed.

She looked over her shoulder to check on him, but he was gone. Confused, she blinked a couple times and focused. Once more, she looked over the side of the bed, trying to find the source of the noise. Not finding him, she sat up as something caught her eye. A foot waved at her from between the mattress and the post of the four-poster bed.

A laugh bubbled up inside of her as she realized what had happened. Rushing to the end of the bed, she peered over to the ground below. Nicolai laid sprawled out on his back after finally extracting his foot from its captive location. A groan of pain escaped his lips, causing laughter to erupt from Mackenzie.

Hearing her laughter, Nicolai soon followed suit, his own ringing through the room. His pride had definitely taken a blow, but the amusement was more prominent. Tears streamed down their faces and breathing took a back seat as they each rolled, one on the ground the other on the bed.

"Oh my God...did you just..." She couldn't finish her question through fits of giggles.

"Oh God..." he exclaimed.

"I can't believe...are you okay?" she questioned, struggling to get words out.

"My pride..." he squeaked, only making them both laugh harder.

"Here...let me..." Her laughter cut off her words once more as she rolled off the bed. Rounding the end, she doubled over at the sight of him naked and prone on the, thankfully, carpeted floor.

She dropped to the floor next to him, unable to stand from the laughter wracking her body. Together, they laid there, gasping for air, not trying in the least to quell their amusement as images of Nicolai's epic back flip off the bed ran through their minds. Mackenzie reached out and held his hand, grounding herself to him in the craziness of the situation.

Eventually, they regained some sort of composure and Nicolai slowly dragged himself from the floor. Reaching a hand down, he easily lifted Mackenzie from the floor and pulled her to him. She giggled as he wrapped his arms around her, leaning in to kiss the hollow at the base of his neck.

"Ready for round two?" she asked playfully.

"Round two?" Shock reverberated from his voice. "Woman...I almost died and you...you're going to be the death of me!"

Through uncontrollable bouts of laughter, they eventually made their way back to the bed and under the covers. Wrapped around each other, they drifted off to sleep with a smile on their faces and giggles on their lips.

Chapter 9

Before he could move an inch, Fiona had spun on her heel and was racing through the house towards the back door.

As her hand closed around the cold, metal door handle, blinding pain sliced through her from behind. Shock stilled every movement and took her breath away.

"Thought you were going to steal from me, bitch?!" he snarled.

She slid silently to the floor, unable to stop her plummet. One burley hand wrapped itself in her hair once more as he drug her through the kitchen and back into the living room. A sickening metallic smell permeated the air and filled her nose while a sticky wetness trailed behind her.

As he stood over her, sneering through his hatred, something inside of Fiona fought for life, giving one last bit of strength to her burning limbs. She kicked out, connecting hard with his shins. He called out in pain, vile obscenities spewing from his mouth. Before her body could muster anything else, however, he stabbed her again. Then again. And again.

Her abdomen burned with each thrust of his knife, pain lacing through every inch of her body. After so long, though, her mind seemed to escape her body just as her blood flowed all around her. Searing pain gave way to weightlessness and her body became blissfully numb. She didn't know how long the assault on her body continued, she didn't even notice when her own life force bubbled up her throat and out of her mouth, trying to strangle her. All she knew was the comforting warmth that seemed to surround her.

***

Mackenzie bolted upright in bed gasping for air. Fear gripped her as she looked around the unfamiliar room before memories of the night before filtered in through the haze of the nightmare. Nicolai. Jaxon. They were one in the same and she was in his room. The image of him sprawled naked on the floor popped into her head, breaking through the fog and bringing a smile to her lips.

She looked beside her, but he was gone. Touching his pillow, her fingers were met with cool temperatures meaning he had been gone for a while. A thought hit her and stole her breath. Had he been there during her nightmare? Had she said something out loud? Is that why he left?

A note on the table by the bed caught her attention and she grabbed it, fighting away the dread building inside.

'Hey beautiful. Sorry to leave you, but I had some calls to make. Not sure if I'll be here when you wake up or not, but you were sleeping so peacefully I didn't want to wake you. Don't worry about leaving, it's safer for you to stay here. There's food in the kitchen and fresh towels in the bathroom. See you soon.'

A sigh of relief left her body as she realized he had missed her nightmare. "Peacefully, huh?" she said to the empty room. Then another thought emerged. "Great. I sleep peacefully while he's here and the moment he leaves, they return. Just great."

She scrubbed her hand over her face to wake up. No matter how wonderful this man was and how well she slept, it couldn't happen again. Not because she regretted any moment of it, but because she couldn't get attached. She was leaving soon.

Sleeping in his arms again would only muddle the already complicated emotions swirling within her further.

Pulling herself out of bed, she made her way to the oversized bathroom. She looked at herself in the mirror and gasped. One blue eye and one green eye stared back at her and bits of red hair peeked out from under the chestnut wig.

"Just another reason to say no to sleepovers. Go to bed Mackenzie and wake up Fiona," she mumbled.

After removing the remaining contact, she jumped in the shower. She took her time basking in the heat and shaking the remainder of the nightmare from her mind. Once the water started to turn cold, she turned it off and stepped out, towel drying her hair and body. She glanced over to her wig and groaned.

"That can't be fixed here," she muttered.

Mackenzie quickly decided that the only course of action was to borrow a car in the garage, hurry home, grab a change of clothes, contacts, wig, etc., and return before Nicolai got back from doing whatever it was he was doing. Plan in mind, she grabbed one of his button up shirts that fell to about mid-thigh on her petit frame and put it on. She called out timidly down the hallway before leaving the room.

Hearing no reply, she quickly made her way down the hall to the stairs in the main foyer. Down the stairs and into the kitchen, her bare feet padded along until something caught her eye and stilled her steps. On the other side of the kitchen was an office with the door wide open. Nicolai sat with his back to the door, but called out to her, nonetheless.

"I was going to go grab some clothes and come right back. Mind if I borrow your car?" Mackenzie replied, trying to keep the rising panic from her voice.

"Sure thing," he responded. Mackenzie exhaled carefully, relieved at his response and his lack of attention. She took a step towards the garage door but stopped in her tracks at his next words. "But before you go, I want to tell you a story."

An indescribable dread clawed its way into her stomach as she nodded her reply to his unseeing back. He must have sensed her response as he continued without waiting.

"I knew this girl once. She was the most incredible girl in the entire world and I was madly in love. To me, she hung the moon and the stars. She was my everything. Her green eyes shined like emeralds when she was happy and flashed like lightening when she was pissed. Her hair was a color rarely seen before, like a mixture of fire and copper, while freckles decorated every inch of her ivory skin."

She closed her eyes as he took a breath. When she reopened them, she found herself moving towards his still turned back. She ached to run to him, to wrap her arms around him, and beg for understanding. The game was up. Yet, he still gave her the chance to run by not looking at her, by not verifying with his own eyes.

"She was my rock. She stood by my side through everything. Every bump and bruise obtained by racing. She nursed me back to health after my motorcycle accident. She gave me confidence and strength, cheering at every baseball game, no matter the outcome. Every fight my parents had, I knew I could count on her to kiss away my tears, to love me in a way they couldn't."

Tears ran down her face as she listed to his view of her and the memories long forgotten resurfaced. Her wig fell from her hand as she shook from the effort it took not to speak.

"She was my best friend. My confidant. My soulmate. I just knew I was going to marry that girl. Everything I did was for her. I lived and breathed for her."

He paused, still never looking back, but knowing she was still there inching closer every second.

"I often wonder what happened to her."

Shock reverberated through her. What had happened to her? Was he serious? Rage bubbled inside of her, squashing all sense of self preservation and need to keep silent.

"You left me!" she shouted, surprising them both by the volume of her outburst.

Slowly, he turned in his chair to face her. His breath caught in his throat at the sight before him. Red hair replaced the brown he had previously seen, hanging loosely around her shoulders. Green eyes flashed at him, expressing her anger and melting his heart.

"It's really you," he whispered, emotion clogging his throat.

"No. You don't get to get emotional! You don't get to look at me like I wounded you!" she demanded, tears flowing unbridled down her face. "You were my world, too, but you left me! No note! No call! Nothing! And I was left to pick up the pieces ALONE!"

Once the dam broke, she could no longer hold back the tide. Years of pain and anger bubbled over and leaked out her eyes. Sobs wracked her body as she slid to the floor and he was immediately on his feet, rushing to her. He fell to his knees before her and scooped her up, crushing her to him.

"I'm so, so sorry. God, Fi...I'm so sorry. I should have fought harder. I should have found a way. I never meant to hurt you." His words were muffled against her damp hair, the sight of her pain undoing his own emotional walls.

Together, they sat on the hardwood floors of the office, clinging to each other through the storm of emotions running through them. Jaxon ran a soothing hand over her hair and back, shushing softly as her tears soaked his shirt. Fiona's hands held tightly to the front of his shirt, afraid that if she let go, he would disappear once more.

What felt like hours later, her tears finally began to run dry, her sobs replaced by hitched breathing and the occasional hiccup. Finally, she pulled her face away from his chest and looked up at him, surprised to see tears on his cheeks as well. Without a second thought, she reached up and brushed them away gently. He smiled softly at her as he did the same for her.

"How long have you known?" she asked, her voice hoarse from crying.

"Officially, today, but I've had my suspicions," he admitted.

Something nagged at her memory. "You said 'still'," she whispered. At his confused expression, she continued. "Last night, you asked if I *still* like it rough."

"I guess in my heart, I knew," he confessed.

"Our hearts and souls knew, even when we didn't," she agreed.

"What about you? When did you know?" he questioned.

"The moment I saw your scar," she said sheepishly. "I'd know that scar anywhere. It has been permanently burned into my brain."

"I knew it," he breathed.

They stared at each other silently, taking in the changes the years had created. They breathed each other in as if they hadn't taken an easy breath in years.

"Jax," she sighed touching his face with the tips of her fingers. "Where did you go? What happened?"

Dread and shame filled his eyes before he hugged her close. He couldn't look at her while he recounted all the memories long buried.

"You know the problems with my parents. You're probably the only one that truly knows, outside of the immediate family. The day we were supposed to meet, I was walking out the door and he blindsided me, sucker punched me with no warning. I was down for the count. There was no fighting back. I was out."

He squeezed her a little tighter as she gasped, needing to comfort her.

"He must have drugged me after, 'cuz when I woke up, we were in Ohio. My phone had been smashed. I was locked in a basement with no way out. It was months before I made my way out of there. By then, he had convinced me that you would hate me for leaving, that you wouldn't take me back. Mom was gone, finally free but nowhere to be found.

"I did the only thing I knew to do, to fully break away and take away any chance of him controlling me. I enlisted in the military and got as far away from that man as possible. I did my four years. I took the most dangerous assignments I could find. But no matter what, every thought returned to you. So...when I got out, I finally grew a pair and I mustered up the courage to find you. No matter what happened, I needed to find you, to see you one more time.

"But when I got there..."

"I was dead," she supplied, saying the words he couldn't.

"I was devastated. I couldn't believe my eyes when I found the article. I couldn't even bring myself to read how it happened, knowing you were gone was bad enough. So, I found a job that would keep me busy, too busy to think...to care...to remember."

"I looked for you, you know," Fiona commented, still curled in his arms. "You were just gone. Your family was gone. I had nothing to go by and the police couldn't do anything. They said your parents had moved and you were still under 18. I, eventually, had to stop looking."

A sob escaped as she buried her face further into his chest. His arms tightened around her, lending her any strength he had left.

"I should have kept looking," she cried. "I never should have stopped."

"Shhhh..." Jaxon cooed. "Stop that. You're not to blame here."

Jaxon cradled her to his chest as he stood up, taking her small frame with him. He took her to the kitchen and sat her on a stool at the bar height island while he moved around the space to make tea. Neither of them said a word as the water heated, staring at it as the tea bags steeped.

"You still like your tea with sweet cream?" he finally asked.

"Yep," she replied softly.

Jaxon finished making the warm drink exactly the way she liked it and sat it in front of her. It served as a peace offering of sorts.

"Want to sit somewhere more comfortable? I feel like this conversation is going to be a while," she chuckled.

Jaxon led them to the living room. Plush couches sat around a coffee table, inviting her in. She sat at one corner, her feet tucked beneath her and her mug of tea in her hands. She wanted to lean on Jaxon for the conversation to come, but knew she couldn't. Dread filled her and she needed to be on her own to tell her story.

"I should have come back sooner," Jaxon muttered as he sat at the other end of the couch, allowing her the distance she needed without being far away.

"Honestly, if you couldn't come back within the first two or three years, it was better this way," she murmured.

"What do you mean?" Confusion filled his voice.

"Your dad was right about one thing. I was angry, bitter even. I thought that maybe you had left because it was all a lie. If you had wanted to, you would have found a way to reach me. I had the stupid thought to date someone else, someone you hated, to make you jealous. I just knew that you hated him so much, that you would *feel* him kiss me and you would run back to me and I would have taken you back in a heartbeat, no questions asked."

She shook her head at her own ignorance. "So, I did. I dated the one man you hated the most."

"Lawrence," he spat, knowing without needing the police report to prove it.

"Lawrence," she confirmed. "I hated his touch, the way he looked at me, but I was too angry at you to leave. I was stupid. Within a year, he asked me to marry him. I said yes for some stupid reason and within a month, we were married. Even then, I would have left him and gone anywhere in the world with you.

"Honestly, we had the perfect, storybook life. With my language skills, I quickly found my way into Linguistics and then International Relations. He, having graduated a few years before us, became a lawyer. He was one of the youngest to ever make partner. By that point, I tried to be happy. Nice house in the suburbs, dream job. Dutiful husband. I had the perfect life on paper. What was not to be happy about?

"That first year, other than me not being in love with him and really only being there out of spite, was perfect." She trailed off, staring into her cup.

"Until it wasn't," he offered, seeing the path she was taking.

"Until it wasn't," she confirmed.

His grip on the mug tightened. He wanted to reach for her, to kiss her, to take it all away, but he knew she needed to do this on her terms. She never was one to be talked into or out of anything.

"What happened?" he finally asked as silence stretched out between them.

She finally raised her eyes to meet his. Something indescribable loomed in her emerald greens.

"Are you sure you want to know? Once I start, there is no turning back," she warned. She held her breath in anticipation of his answer. Part of her wanted to clamp a lid on Pandora's box and run away, but part of her needed to tell her story, to share the burden with her once true love.

"I'm here for whatever and however you want to tell me," he told her, settling in on the couch more.

Fiona took a deep breath, trying to calm her nerves. "If you're sure..." she paused once more, giving him a chance to back out. "In that case, hold on tight."

Chapter 10

8 years earlier

She smoothed her hand over the fabric of her dark pencil skirt as her stilettos clicked across the tile floors. In her other hand, clutched tightly, was an Olive Garden bag containing lunch for two. Fiona knew her husband hated surprise visits, but lately he had been avoiding her at every turn and today was too important. She had news to tell him and she didn't think she could wait for him to get home. Instead, she used her lunch hour from the International Relations firm she worked for to surprise him.

Looking around the law firm her husband ran, she was curious at the complete lack of people. Obviously, it was lunch hour, but there were usually still some poor souls rushing around to finish something for a case they had been assigned. It made her question if the firm was doing as well as she had been led to believe or if something had happened. Fiona filed it away to ask her husband another time. Today was not the day for such conversations.

The elevator ride was a silent one, as even the boring music that usually played was out to lunch it seemed. Her shoe tapped out her impatience as she shifted the bag to her other hand. The floor numbers pinged by at a snail's pace as she made her way to the top floor of the high rise that helped define the Atlanta skyline. As she finally ran out of numbers above the door, she took a deep steadying breath as she waited on the doors to open.

Natural light met her eyes as she stepped out of the metal box. Executive floor. Owners suites. Only the best for the privileged men and women on this floor. Her smile faltered a bit as, again, the usually bustling hall was devoid of all human presence. Just as before, she pushed the uneasiness aside. Not today.

As she reached her intended door, she paused once more. Breathing deeply to steady her shaking hands, she renewed the smile on her face and ran her free hand through her copper-red hair. Exhaling her held breath, she opened his door and stepped inside with more confidence than she suddenly felt.

"Oh Lawrence, honey! I know you hate when I don't call ahead," she called out in a sing-song voice. "But I was in the area and decided to grab lunch!" She continued through the outer office to his private area in the back. Hearing his voice, she opened the inner door. "Lawre-"

Her words were cut off by a quiet popping noise and what sounded like a bag of bricks being dropped on the floor. Four men, not including her husband, stood around what appeared to be a crumbled man in a cheap suit laying on the ground. In her husband's hand was a literal smoking gun, a silencer attached to the end.

The bag of take-out clattered to the tile floor as shock overtook her body. Her eyes widened to the point of being painful and blood rushed to her ears. She stared at the body on the floor, trying to create a rational scenario in her muddled mind that didn't involve her husband shooting it dead. Her mouth hung open and an audible gasp escaped her lips.

"Fiona?" Lawrence questioned, breaking the silence.

Her eyes scanned the room once more before landing on her husband. She had never seen the other men in the room or the look in her husband's eyes before. He looked mad enough to add her to the pile on the floor. She fought to form thoughts as she stared at him, fear clawing through her body.

"Oh, silly me," she began, hating the tremble in her voice. "I forgot drinks."

Before anyone else could react, she was sprinting out of his office and down the empty halls. She slid to a stop at the elevators as her hand frantically hit the down button over and over, praying the doors would open in time. Voices reached her ears as tears began to gather in her eyes.

"Come on! Come on!" she begged, willing the silver doors to open.

Blissfully, the doors opened as the first person emerged from Lawrence's office. She shot through the opening before it was generally wide enough to do so and reached for the buttons within. She slammed her hand into the main lobby button before repeatedly tapping the door close button. Thankfully, before the doors fully opened, they were already closing.

Air rushed from her lungs as she leaned against the back wall. Her mind raced to put the pieces together, to rationalize what she had seen as her eyes glued themselves to the numbers over the silver doors. Was her husband part of the mob? She knew, being a defense attorney, he dealt with less than stellar people, but had he really fallen so far? How long had this been going on? She knew they had their issues, but how had she been so blind?

The questions kept coming as the numbers dropped, and with them, her realistic expectations of getting out of this alive. She prayed that, as slow as this death trap was, it was faster than one of those men racing down the stairs. She decided she needed a plan, to think through her next logical steps.

Step one, run like hell. Step two, once outside, use automatic start on her car. Step three, drive like a maniac. It seemed overly simplistic and not very thought out, but that was as far as she could get at that moment. She would plan more once her car was far enough away that this building no longer reflected in her rear-view mirror.

The chime for the main floor rang through the lobby and the doors began inching open. She pulled as much air into her lungs as possible, preparing for the race of her life. Without looking around to see if anyone had beat her to her escape, she sprang from the barely open doors and ran like the devil himself was chasing her.

She hadn't made it halfway across the lobby when her stilettos betrayed her and dropped her hard to the solid marble floors. Pain radiated through her knee, pulling a hiss from between her clenched teeth. Ripping her traitorous shoes from her feet, she flung them away from her and clamored to her feet once more.

She burst through the glass panel doors into the hot, humid Atlanta air. She dug her keys from the purse slung across her body as her bare feet ate up the hot expanse of the sidewalk before her. Her engine roared to life in front of her, giving her impossible escape a little hope.

Her hands grappled with the handle of the driver's side door before flinging the door open and jumping inside. Her hand flew to the lock button as if that would stop bullets from piercing her temporary sanctuary. Throwing the car in reverse, she backed out of her parking spot before squealing her tires as she lurched forward, leaving the nightmare firmly behind her.

She gripped the steering wheel tightly to stop her hands from shaking. The blast of A/C on her face helped clear her mind as she wove in and out of traffic, hoping she wasn't pulled over for speeding by God's Special People. The lull of traffic and lack of obvious psycho stalker in her rear-view gave her a moment to think somewhat rationally.

She had to run. It was as clear as the sky above her head. She would not be safe anywhere in this city or even the state. She probably needed to leave the south all together to even have a chance of surviving. Life as she knew it was over, but there was still one thing left to do.

"Hey Google, call Jade," she stated as tears began to slide down her cheeks. She didn't trust her hands enough to leave the steering wheel long enough to brush them away, so they fell unhindered.

What felt like an eternity passed before the line clicked in response.

"Jade! It's Fi! I-"

"Hey, it's Jade. Sorry I missed your call-"

"Damn it!" Fiona screamed as her best friend's voice mail message came across the line. "Of all the times, Jade."

As the pre-recoded message came to a close, she took a deep breath and steadied her voice. Leaving a message wouldn't help if it was incomprehensible.

"Hey Jade, it's Fi," she began as calmly as possible. "I have to go out of town for a while and I don't know when I'll be back. Don't look for me and don't tell anyone I called. Watch your back. I love you." Her voice cracked over her final words and she quickly disconnected the line.

She hated the cryptic tone of the call, but it couldn't be helped. She wouldn't risk her friend's safety by telling her more. She knew she would likely never see her again, or her own parents for that matter, and her heart broke all over again. How had her life come to this?

"Snap out of it, Fi!" she verbally assaulted herself. "Think dammit!"

She drug herself out of her pity party and focused on her next steps. She knew that going home was risky, but she didn't have much of a choice. She wouldn't get far on fumes and dreams. She needed cash, lots of cash, and some clean clothes wouldn't hurt. Her mental check list ticked off in her mind as she pulled into her blissfully empty driveway.

Flying out of her still running car, she entered the code quickly on her electronic locks and burst into the house of lies. Everything about this house was built on the misconception of her husband being a good man. The wedding pictures she passed as she raced up the stairs, the bed they shared that she ran into as she flew to the closet, all of it was a lie. If she was honest, even her love for him was a lie. At least that made her next move easier to fathom.

Her fingers flew over the keypad of the safe and the door popped open with a satisfying click. Grabbing the nearest bag to her, she shoveled stacks of cash into it, nearly emptying everything they had saved. Jumping to her feet, she rummaged through her clothes, grabbing only what she needed to get to wherever she was going. She could buy more once she got there, but business attire wasn't exactly practical for being on the run.

Deciding she would change whenever she stopped for gas, she closed her bag and exited the closet. Bag slung over her shoulder, she ran down the carpeted stairs and into the living room. Her entire body was on alert as she crossed into the kitchen. Flinging open one of the drawers, she rummaged through the junk inside until her fingers felt the cool steel of the one thing she was looking for.

Realistically, Fiona knew a knife was no match for a bullet, but it was all she had. She hurried back to the living room in search for her keys. Finding her flip flops along the way, she wracked her brain trying to remember where she had put them. She mentality retraced her steps from the moment she had arrived five point two five minutes ago.

She face palmed herself as she realized her mistake. They were still in the car, which was still running. Her speedy get away awaited just outside. She sprinted to the front door, her flip flops click clacking on her feet, and flung open the front door.

Ice water ran through her veins as her eyes fell on the suit clad man before her. Her mind simultaneously raced and emptied of all thought as his lips curled into a menacing smile. She staggered backwards, trying to put space between the two of them as her eyes darted around, looking for any way out.

"You should have called," his icy voice cooed as he stalked towards her. "You know I hate unscheduled visits at the office."

Her hands shook. Her breathing ceased. Her impending death loomed over her in the form of her pillar-of-the-community-turned-murderer husband. The man who had promised to love, honor, and cherish her three short years prior was now to be her end. It gave an entirely new meaning to 'till death do us part' and somehow, the irony was not lost on her.

"Sorry, I got called to Washington by a client. It was all very sudden and I...uh...just wanted to say bye in person before leaving for the airport," she lied, trying to keep her voice as steady as possible. Maybe, if he thought someone was expecting her, he would let her leave as to not raise suspicion.

His raised eyebrow as he peered at her choice of luggage for an 'official' business trip made her heart stop. It didn't exactly scream 'International Relations Guru' and he wasn't buying it. Still, she kept going. This was her only shot and she had to get outside.

"I couldn't find my suitcase and my favorite suit hasn't been dry cleaned. I just threw some essentials in a bag and figured I would go shopping once I got to New York. You don't mind if I use the credit card, do you?" she asked, trying to sound rational.

"Sure honey, I don't mind," he crowed, moving to the side, giving her a glimpse of freedom. "We'll talk when you get back."

Relief rushed through her as she stepped towards the door. Escape was within her grasp. She fought down the vomit that threated to spew as she raised on her tip toes to give what she hoped was a loving kiss on the cheek.

She stepped on the porch as air breathed into her body. Willing herself not to bolt, she tried to control her racing heart.

"Oh, one thing," Lawrence stated, making her steps falter. "I thought you were going to Washington."

Terror washed over her from head to toe. Why would she be shopping in New York if she was going to Washington? The gig was up. There was only one thing left to do.

She lurched forward, ready to run for her life. Her scream was cut off in her throat as her forward momentum was halted. His hands tangled in her hair, yanking her backwards off her feet. Her hands shot to his in an attempt to relieve the pain caused by her red hair being removed from her scalp, strand by agonizing strand. Her feet fought to find traction on the hard concrete, anything at all to stop her from being pulled back into that house.

With one final tug, he threw her small frame into the house. The engine in her car was still running and the driver's door was still open. Her flip flops lay haphazardly on the porch. Those were the only signs that anything was amiss as the view of the outside world was taken away by the closing of the door and the click of the lock.

Her head snapped to the left as pain exploded in her cheek bone. Ringing sounded in her ears as spots danced before her eyes. Her hand gingerly touched the assaulted area in an attempt to comprehend what was happening.

Lawrence didn't even have the audacity to look sorry for striking her, or that he even felt the impact of the blow himself. How many other people had he hit in such a way as to no longer feel the sting of flesh against flesh? Who was this monster before her and how had she not seen the truth?

"How much did you see, Fiona?" he asked menacingly, removing his coat jacket carefully.

"Only that I interrupted a meeting with who I can only guess were clients. I...I was startled. I realize now, I didn't clean up the mess from our lunch on your floor. I'm truly sorry," she stammered.

"So you didn't see the dead body on the floor?" he joked, already knowing the answer.

Fiona scrambled to her feet, needing to regain some kind of ground in the upcoming fight for her life. She knew that if he was admitting to the dead body that he didn't intend for her to make it out alive.

"Why would I see a dead body? Why would there be a dead body in your office? Tha...that's just crazy," she stammered, backing away.

"Of course! That's not why you're leaving is it?" he goaded, stepping closer.

"Absolutely not! I take my work very seriously," she played along, clutching her bag as tightly as she could.

His eyes slid over her and landed at her bag. Before she could move fast enough to get out of reach, his hand clamped onto the strap of her makeshift luggage. He pulled hard, ripping the fabric in two as her belongings toppled to the floor.

Anger flared inside of him as the stacks of cash landed on top. She could almost see the steam puffing out of his ears as his face almost instantly turned red. Before he could move an inch, Fiona had spun on her heel and was racing through the house towards the back door.

As her hand closed around the cold, metal door handle, blinding pain sliced through her from behind. Shock stilled every movement and took her breath away.

"Thought you were going to steal from me, bitch?!" he snarled.

She slid silently to the floor, unable to stop her plummet. One burley hand wrapped itself in her hair once more as he drug her through the kitchen and back into the living room. A sickening metallic smell permeated the air and filled her nose while a sticky wetness trailed behind her.

As he stood over her, sneering through his hatred, something inside of Fiona fought for life, giving one last bit of strength to her burning limbs. She kicked out, connecting hard with his shins. He called out in pain, vile obscenities spewing from his mouth. Before her body could muster anything else, however, he stabbed her again. Then again. And again.

Her abdomen burned with each thrust of his knife, pain lacing through every inch of her body. After so long, though, her mind seemed to escape her body just as her blood flowed all around her. Searing pain gave way to weightlessness and her body became blissfully numb. She didn't know how long the assault on her body continued, she didn't even notice when her own life force bubbled up her throat and out of her mouth, trying to strangle her. All she knew was the comforting warmth that seemed to surround her.

Memories drifted through her mind. Memories of a time when she had been deeply loved by a man. A time before he had left her to this fate. Jaxon. The name whispered across her raw nerve endings, comforting her, helping her escape. She wanted to stay in that moment forever, his smile, his kiss, his touch, but something else was tugging at her, trying to break through.

Banging sounded around her, light at first, then louder, closer, more insistent. Her eyes fluttered open lazily as her mind tried to sort through what was happening. It was dark now, no sun light came through the windows. A muffled voice called to her from somewhere outside. Her cell phone rang nearby. As she tried to look around, pain laced through her body and the memory of the assault came rushing back.

Panic rose within her. She tried to call out for help, but words would not form. She closed her eyes against the pain and fear, praying it was all just a dream. She tried to return to Jaxon. She wanted to see his mischievous smirk again, but couldn't quite get there. When her eyes finally opened once more, worried brown eyes stared back at her. Light brown hair framed the face that was now inches from her own.

"Please hurry! She's still alive!" her best friends voice screamed into what Fiona could only guess was a cell phone. "Stay with me, Fi! I swear to God if you die on me, I WILL kill you!"

Fiona tried to laugh at such an absurd idea but only succeeded in forcing more blood through her lips and down her chin. Jade screamed more at the person on the phone but Fiona couldn't make out anything more that was said. Red lights began to flash around her as her eyes closed once more.

Fiona jolted awake, her eyes flying open, pulling her from yet another memory of her time with Jaxon, this time they had been together on a beach for Spring Break. Instantly regretting that decision, she squeezed them shut against the bright lights. Sounds of the world around her began to filter in. A machine beeped nearby. Voices whispered further away. Someone breathed deeply next to her. Where was she? What was that incessant beeping?

Slowly this time, she peeked her eyes open, letting them adjust to the light. Stark white walls met her with blinding overhead lights. Her mouth was dry as she slowly rolled her head to the side. Long brown hair cascaded over the rails of Fiona's bed. The deep breathing was from her best friend asleep beside her.

"Ja-" Her voice was raspy, either from lack of use or from dehydration, she wasn't sure which. She cleared her throat and tried again. "Jade."

Chestnut hair flew through the air as Jade came alive beside her. Her brown eyes rimmed with unshed tears as she stared at Fiona in shock.

"You look like hell," Fiona joked when Jade stared at her without saying a word.

"Me?!" Jade responded laughing, pulling from her stupor. "Have you looked in a mirror?"

Fiona winced in pain when a giggle bubbled within her. "I don't know how I look, but I feel like I've been to hell and back. What happened? Was I in an accident?"

"You don't remember?" Jade asked, her eyes expanding once more. "I guess that could be a blessing."

"Darling! You're awake!"

That voice. It washed over her like ice water and with it came the memory of what happened. All of it in painful detail. Jade must have seen the truth in Fiona's eyes because she shifted uncomfortably in her seat, her eyes sliding between husband and wife.

Fiona slowly turned towards the voice, praying against all odds that her mind was playing some sick joke. There he was, in all his glory. He was playing the perfect, doting husband, worried sick about his adoring wife. He was clean of all outward evidence of his crimes, but Fiona could see her blood all over him.

Her heart rate rose, and with it, the speed of the beeping nearby. Leave it to the stupid machine to give her away. Her breathing shallowed as he rushed to her side. Tears of 'joy' rolled down his face. His smile meant only for her. He was good. Fiona realized now how he had fooled her. He was a master of this.

"Okay everyone, let's let our patient get some air. We need to lower that heart rate and take some vitals. This is the most excitement she's had in a week and we don't want to overdo it," an unfamiliar male voice instructed.

Fiona's eyes flicked to Jade, then back to Lawrence, afraid to let him out of her sight. Jade reluctantly moved towards the door, glancing back and forth between the 'happy' couple. A determined look came over Jade's face.

"I'll be back as soon as they let me," Jade promised, then disappeared into the hallway.

Lawrence bent down and kissed Fiona on the forehead as he had done a thousand times before. This time, however, she had to forcefully restrain herself from flinching.

"I know you remember," he whispered in her ear. "If you tell anyone anything, I'll kill your family. Then, I'll finish what I started with you."

His venom laced words made her want to vomit. To anyone watching, he was comforting his wife who he thought he had lost. To Fiona, it was a death sentence.

With what seemed like one last loving glance, he called out "I love you," before he left the room.

Chapter 11

Jaxon stared at Fiona as she recalled the day that changed her life. Her eyes were a swirl of emotions as she lost herself to the memories that threatened to suffocate the life out of her. He physically hurt for her, hearing what she had gone through, what that man had done to her, to HIS Fiona. He understood why she had tried to distance herself from him once she heard he was with the Mafia. That kind of life had already destroyed so much of her.

Looking down, he placed his now empty mug on the table as the real concern of smashing it with his bare hands took root. He wanted to punch something, to shout and yell. He wanted to find Lawrence and kill him slowly. He also wanted to hold Fiona close and never let go. She looked so lost, so frail. She had obviously gone to great lengths to reinvent herself, make her body a weapon on its own in an attempt to protect herself. Even so, seeing her like this, she looked broken.

"So, that's why you faked your death," he offered when she had stayed silent for longer than usual.

"Yes..." she replied, blinking away the memories. "And no. I learned later that Jade had immediately gone to the police. She knew the moment she saw me with Lawrence that he had done it. There was no question in her mind. Before I could tell her not to, it was done.

"The moment the police questioned Lawrence, my parents' fate was sealed. I convinced the doctors to release me the day of their funeral. Standing there in that graveyard, I knew what I had to do. I couldn't bury my best friend. I couldn't lose Jade. She was all I had left. Once the service was over, I drove straight to the police station.

"I found the detective in charge of my case, the one Jade had spoken to, and I made a deal. I would tell them everything, cooperate in any way necessary, but Jade's name had to be removed from everything. No mention of her whatsoever. It was the only way I knew to truly keep her safe. Only three people knew it had been her. I made sure it stayed that way.

"I testified. I told all I knew. I gave access to everything we owned. I listened to the trial as his lawyers tried to paint him as an upstanding member of society while making me out to be a whore. Somehow, this was my fault. My punishment for...something. At the end of it all, I hugged Jade good-bye and started a new life in witness protection. Jade accepted the life insurance policy pay out that Lawrence had taken out on me and put it away, just in case."

"So, you're still in witsec?" Jaxon asked, not remembering that from the report.

"No. I was only there a few weeks before he found me. Letters started flowing in. Some vile, some begging me to forgive him. They moved me a couple times, but it didn't matter. He always found me. That's when we faked my death. I had divorced Lawrence during the trial, but this was the last hold he had on my life. I had to die."

"Does Jade know? That you're alive, I mean?"

"Yeah, only her, the detective, and now you. I was actually on the phone with her when we met...and when I got roped into that other date you rescued me from," she admitted.

"That makes so much more sense now," Jaxon smirked. "You two always were crazy when you got together. The Dangerous Duo, as I remember."

"I miss her so much," Jade commented sadly.

"Do you ever go back?"

"No. Not while he's alive. I can't. I have access to the insurance policy, so I have money. I move around at least once a year, sometimes more if things seem wrong. I can't afford to stay in one place for long. But no matter where I go, I train. I won't be so easy to take down again. I won't be a victim to anyone ever again."

Jaxon moved closer to her on the couch for the first time since they sat down. He wrapped his hands around hers and her eyes finally met his. "You're not a victim. You're a survivor," he said gently.

"That's what they all say," she said with a humorless laugh, "but the truth is, I never should have gone home that day. I never should have gone for the cash, even if it was both of ours, and I should have fought instead of ran. I was a victim that day, but never again."

The conviction in her voice tore at him. Fiona was, in some ways, the same girl he fell in love with all those years ago. In many other ways, however, she would never be the same.

"Why did you think of me?" he finally found the courage to ask. "Through the worst of it, why me?"

"Isn't it obvious?" Fiona asked, blinking at him in confusion. "You were my happy place, the one thing that could get me through the darkness."

Unable to hold himself back any longer, Jaxon pulled her to him, wrapping his arms around her and holding her tight. Even after he had abandoned her to that monster, she had still thought of him. It had been the same for him, but he thought she might have moved on by then.

"If you knew it was me last night, then why the boundaries? Why the rules? Why did you feel like you had to keep your shirt on?" he wondered, not easing up on his hold on her.

"The scars," she answered softly.

"Of course," he cursed himself for not figuring it out. "The anxiety, the PTSD, it all makes sense. Was this the first time you...I mean...since he..."

"Yes," she whispered. "I can't let anyone close. I can't usually stand anyone touching me at all, much less..."

"Do you still have nightmares?" he questioned, thinking over his experience with his military buddies who had suffered trauma.

"Every night," she confirmed.

"But not last night?" He thought back over the night and didn't remember anything happening.

"After you left." She snuggled deeper into his embrace, breathing him in. "Apparently, having you near keeps the boogey man away."

Gently, he guided her face to meet is gaze. Slowly, slightly afraid she might disappear, he inched his face closer to hers. When their lips met, the kiss was soothing, reassuring, conveying thoughts and emotions that neither of them could put into words. When they finally broke apart, he rested his forehead against hers. He steeled himself for the question that was on his mind.

"Can I see them?"

She stilled in his arms and her breathing stopped. She knew he would want to see them, but she still wasn't prepared to hear the words. If there was anyone she ever trusted enough to show them to, it was him. Still, she hesitated. How would he react? Would he pity her? Would he get angry? Something in between? Which would be easier to handle?

She pulled herself out of the warmth of his arms and moved across the room before she lost her nerve. As she slowly undid each button of his shirt, she paced. She tried to breathe through the inevitable panic, forcing herself to take slow, deep breaths. She vaguely noticed him move to the edge of the couch, watching her every move.

She stopped pacing as his shirt fell from her shoulders, pooling at her feet. Standing before him, she took one last deep breath and closed her eyes. She couldn't bring herself to watch him as he looked over her. Slowly, she peeled her cami off over her head, dropping it to the floor as well. Her armor was gone and she was left bare for all to see.

Her heartbeat pounded in her ears as she waited. Silence met her, raising her anxiety even more. Just as she thought he might never speak, he let out a primal shout and she heard the coffee table slam into the wall and shatter.

Anger. She should have known anger would be his first response. Flinching at the sound of wood smashing, she still kept her eyes closed. She knew where he was in his mind. She had been there, too. She didn't need to see it to be reminded.

Her eyes fluttered open when his hands softly caressed her hips. He was kneeling in front of her, tears streaking down his cheeks as his fingers whispered across each scar. Some were barely visible anymore, others were still puckered and obvious, but all were felt by her soul.

"I should have come back immediately, called...something. None of this would have happened if I..." his voice trailed off, thick with emotion.

"I shouldn't have been so angry, so bitter. I should have known you would come back to me as soon as you were able. It's just as much my fault as yours," she told him, sliding to her knees, eye to eye with him.

"This wasn't your fault!" he protested, shocked she would even think that.

"Then stop blaming yourself, too."

He knew she was right. Pain and guilt gnawed at him in the pit of his stomach and he had to fight the urge to vomit. His Fiona, his beautiful Fiona, had been assaulted by a mad man with a knife. He knew he should have controlled his emotions better, throwing the table had been too much, but as he stared at the marks on her body, he knew there was no way to fully hide the pain within.

"I thought I was prepared," he began, his voice low. "I read the police report. I saw the photos. It wasn't enough. Nothing could have prepared me for this."

"You knew?" she gasped. "You knew and you still asked me to tell it?"

"Yes," he admitted, meeting her accusing gaze. "I needed to hear it from you, to hear your version. Police reports are all facts, no emotion. And I needed you to trust me enough to tell me."

Fiona stared at him in shock. She wanted to be angry, but she wasn't. He had let her tell her story instead of trusting someone else's version. He trusted her more than a piece of paper. She softly brushed his tears aside, giving him a weak smile.

"Thank you," she whispered. "Even at my trial, my story was rehearsed, edited. This is the first time I've been able to tell it my way, at my pace."

Jaxon nodded in response, unable to trust his voice before his attention returned to her scars. He slowly lowered himself to a fully sitting position to get a better look. One in particular caught his attention and his stomach dropped. He ran his thumb over it, forcing the bile threating to climb its way out, back down.

"There is one thing not in the report...and you didn't say it either," he said softly.

She swallowed down the fear inside her. She knew what he was going to ask. He was the only one to ever catch it, to truly hear her words. He would be the only one to ever know. She nodded her encouragement.

"What was the good news you were going to tell him?"

She willed herself to say the words she had never told a soul. "I was pregnant."

The words hung heavily in the air between them even if they were barely heard. She could see his mind racing as he fought to come to terms with what she had said. She knew the instant he had asked that he already knew the answer.

Without a word, he leaned forward and kissed the scar just below her belly button, the one that had told him his answer even before he had asked. He was torn in so many directions. He didn't want that man's child inside of her, but he didn't want that loss for her either. He was ashamed that through the pain, he also was relieved, relieved she didn't have to carry the child of the man who was capable of doing something so horrible.

"I thought that maybe, a child could pull us together, make me happy. But when the doctors told me I had...it was...well, I only felt relief. Relieved that I didn't have to look at that tiny face and see Lawrence." Sobs wracked her body as he pulled her onto his lap. "I would have loved that child no matter what, but it wouldn't have been fair to him or her. It wouldn't have been the same. It wouldn't have been yours."

His heart shattered at her words. Even with everything she had gone though, everything she had lost, her thoughts were of him. He couldn't believe how incredible she was, how selfless. He had no words, no ability to express the myriad of emotions he was feeling. Instead he just held her as they both cried for a past best forgotten and a future that never was.

***

The sun had set by the time either of them attempted to move. No more words had been spoken but plenty of tears had been shed as they clung to one another sitting on the living room floor. Fiona had finally allowed herself to break, to let it all out in a way other than in a boxing ring, and Jaxon had been lost in thought as he held her close.

"I have to say," she chuckled, finally breaking the silence. "You've definitely filled out."

The low rumble of his laughter revived her broken soul. "Are you checking me out?" he teased.

"From the moment you ran into me in that coffee shop," she admitted. "But now, knowing it's you...I mean, damn."

"And what about you?" he asked, his laughter louder now. "You were always the most beautiful woman I had ever seen, but now? Now these curves are lethal!"

Her giggles joined his and some of the tension finally lifted in the room.

"I guess we've both grown up a bit," she conceded.

"So, I have to know," he started, the mischievous glint back in his eye. "That dream you had in my car that first night. Did the real thing live up to your fantasy or did it fall flat?"

"Oh honey," she giggled. "Considering the dream never made it past kissing, you could say the real deal did back flips in comparison."

The mention of Jaxon's epic dismount from the bed had them both breathless with laughter once more. They each had to fight hard to squash that image down enough to catch their breath.

"For you, I'll backflip any time. But maybe next time, let's find some mats to land on," he suggested playfully.

"Deal," she agreed, interrupted by her stomach rumbling. "Maybe for now we can get some food. I don't remember the last time I ate."

"Well, we can't have that, now can we?" he teased. Finally standing, he helped her off the floor and wrapped his shirt around her once more.

"What?" she asked, looking at the goofy grin on his face.

"I love seeing you in my clothes," he confessed.

A faint blush tinged her cheeks as she looked down at herself in his shirt. "Was there ever anyone else? After me, I mean?"

"No."

Her eyes flew to his at the finality of his response. "No one?"

"I tried a couple times, but no one was you. I eventually stopped. I dated a few times under cover, just to keep up my image, but nothing beyond dinner and drinks. That's all that was supposed to have been with you, too, but obviously that didn't happen."

"It's like we knew..." she stopped herself from continuing her thought. "So...food?"

His laughter warmed her. "You always did have a one-track mind when it came to being hungry."

"What can I say? Some things never change."

Hand in hand, they made their way to the kitchen. Fiona took the offered stool at the bar while Jaxon decided on what to fix. It wasn't long before the smell of pasta filled the air as an Americanized form of spaghetti was prepared with all the love and laughter of two souls being reunited.

"I forgot how sexy it is to watch you cook," Fiona mused from her vantage point.

"Oh really? I didn't think you could forget something like that," he joked.

"Har har har...just take the compliment and move on," she sassed.

"Well then, thank you, and dinner is served."

Together, they moved to the eating nook off the side of the kitchen, bringing plates of food, wine, and salad with them. They nestled in next to one another and continued filling each other in on the gap of time they were apart.

Fiona couldn't help but feel content, like part of her had been missing but had finally been returned. It had been so long since she had done something so normal as have a homecooked meal with someone she knew, and even longer with someone she was in love with. She let go of the uncertainty of tomorrow and let herself live in the moment.

She watched as he sat back casually, the easy confidence that he embodied rolled off of him, setting her at ease. It was like they had never been apart, like the years in between had magically been erased, cleansed. She was happy for the first time in as long as she could remember, content. She loved hearing that his mom had gotten out and that they had eventually reconnected, even as it made her long for her own.

"So, I have to ask, why wigs and not just dye your hair? It has to be easier," Jaxon commented, breaking through her nostalgic moment.

"You know me, I couldn't mess with the red."

The twinkle in her eye set his body on fire. She was the only woman he had ever met to set him off with a single look. Sitting here with her, after believing she was lost for such a long time, was a dream come true and his body was unable to contain that excitement. Every move she made was seductive, she didn't even have to try. Just being near her was going to be his undoing.

He forced himself to focus on her answer about her hair. He knew how much she loved her hair color. He also knew that she remembered how much he loved her red hair. He reached out and ran a hand through it thoughtfully.

"I've been alone for so long, my red hair just reminded me of you," she shrugged. "I couldn't get rid of that part of me."

"Well, you aren't alone anymore," he promised.

The look that entered her eyes as she looked at him made him pause. His smile faltered as hers fell. Apprehension filled him as she opened her mouth to speak.

"Jax, I love you," she told him, tears welling up in her eyes.

"I love you too, Fi. Why does it feel like there is a 'but' in there?" he asked carefully.

"I...I can't stay much longer in Italy. Someone is...looking into me, it seems. It's not safe for me to stay," she admitted cautiously.

"Who? Is that what you weren't telling me last night? Did the Don say something?" Concern for her safety scooted him closer to her.

"Yes."

"Don't worry, he won't be an issue much longer," he assured her.

"The damage is still done. He's looking. You've looked. Too many people in this area are looking into my past. He obviously has friends in high places. It won't take long for it to get back to Lawrence. I have to go." Her words were soft but confident.

Jaxon knew she was right, it would be suspicious. "Okay...where will you go? I'll follow you later when I can."

"I c-can't tell you that..." Tears began spilling over and sliding down her cheeks.

"What do you mean? I just found you again, I have no intention of losing you!" Panic began welling up in his chest. She was going to run and he was going to lose her all over again.

"I want nothing more than to be with you, but you're a cop."

"What does that have to do with the price of tea in China?" he questioned, his voice betraying his fear.

"We faked my death. Insurance was paid. I'm technically a fugitive. Even if I wanted to return, if he was no longer an issue, you're a cop and I broke the law."

Realization washed over him like a bucket of ice water. She was right. By law, he should be reporting her to his superiors. Just looking into her folder was enough to tip someone off, but luckily, he could play it off as having known her, just wanting to know what happened to her. Even if he could protect her from her ex, he would have to choose between her and his oath.

"This is exactly why I wasn't going to tell you who I was, even when I knew it was you. I never wanted you to have to choose. And I didn't want to hurt you when I left," she told him, reading his mind.

"We can figure this out. There has to be a way to fix this," he muttered, desperately looking for a solution he could live with.

"Not before I have to leave, maybe not even before I was thrown in jail where he could reach me easier. I'm sorry, but this is the only way."

"No! I can't live with that!" he shouted, jumping up from the table.

"You don't have much of a choice," she reminded him. "I hate it, too, but I won't make you choose. And I won't risk him finding me."

"No! Just no! I-" his words were cut off by the ringing of his phone in his office. "Damn it!" he cursed. "I have to take this. I'm so sorry. I'll just be a second."

He ran to answer the phone, cursing at the person on the other end. After a few moments, he returned to the table. His expression was dark and guarded.

"I have to go. Please...please don't leave. Not yet. Give me a week to finish this job and figure some things out. That's all I'm asking. One week," he begged.

"Jax-" she began, her heart breaking.

"Please. One week!" He pulled her to her feet and wrapped his arms around her. "Promise me."

He crushed his lips to hers, desperate to convince her to let him try. Heat and passion surged through them both as they clung to one another.

"Promise me!" he demanded between kisses.

"One week," she conceded.

His victorious smile melted her heart, even as she knew she would regret her decision.

Chapter 12

Fiona, disguised as Mackenzie once more, stepped onto the street, leaving the gym after a great sparring session, possibly her last. She had promised Jaxon one week, and there were only three days left. She hadn't heard a word from him since he had left after getting the phone call. She wasn't sure if she had hoped to see him before the week was up or not. Part of her needed to see him one last time, but part of her knew it would never be enough.

It hadn't been all bad, though. She had used that time to scope out her next location and get a feel of the land. She had chosen a new name, a new identity. She had even checked in on Elise after the scare at the concert, giving her resignation with an excuse of unsavory patrons. She had started packing and selling things in her apartment, even getting her new passport in order.

If Jaxon couldn't figure out in the next three days how to keep her out of jail AND safe, she was gone. She had no other choice.

A smile spread across her face as her phone rang and she saw the name that appeared.

"Jade!" she greeted. "Boy do I have a lot to tell you!"

"Fiona..." Jade's voice was low, laced with fear.

"Jade, you know you can't-"

"I know Fi, but I need your attention."

"Okay, it's obviously bad. Lay it on me." Fiona focused on her long-time best friends voice preparing for the worst.

"It's Lawrence. He's escaped."

The world around her slowed to a stop. Her breath refused to fill her lungs and her feet refused to move. It was happening. The threat was real and Lawrence was coming for her.

"Fi?" Jade called, pulling her from her thoughts.

"How long ago?" Fiona asked, her mind jumping from standing still to overdrive. Her feet now sprinted towards home.

"A week. He killed the detective. That's why I didn't know before now. I think he might be...I'm afraid he's..."

"He's coming for me," Fiona finished for her, knowing Jade couldn't bring herself to say the words.

"I think so...I can't find out much without giving away that you're alive. I've tried. I don't know how he found out. I don't even know how much time you have..." Her words trailed off.

"I know, Jade. I need you to get away for a few days, just to be safe."

"I could go-"

"No...don't tell me," Fiona interrupted. "I don't need to know. And don't keep this number. I'll reach out to you when I can."

"Fiona, wait!" Jade called out.

"I have to go, Jade. Take care of you. I'll be in touch soon."

Fiona disconnected the line before Jade could protest any more. She knew she needed to ditch the phone, but there was one last thing she needed to do. Someone she needed to call. She took a deep breath in preparation for the argument to come. There was no way around it. She pressed the button on her phone to call.

The line rang and rang. Her heartbeat faster with each passing second that he didn't answer. She let out her held breath when the voice mail answered instead.

"Niko," she began. "Jax," she corrected lovingly. "I'm so so sorry. I know I promised. I know you still have three days left. I wish I could tell you instead of your voicemail, but maybe it's better this way. I have to leave. Today. Now. I'll be gone by the time you get this. He found me...he's on his way. I don't have a choice. I love you. I'll always love you. Don't look for me, you won't find me. I love you Jaxon. Good-bye."

She clicked the line off as tears ran down her face. She knew this day would come, but she wasn't prepared. She would never be prepared. She took a moment to compose herself before forcing herself to move forward once more. She could nurse her broken heart with a bottle of tequila later, but first, she had to stay alive.

She propelled herself forward, racing home to grab her go bag. Normally, she kept it in her car so she never had to return home if this situation arose, but she never got a car after moving the last time. She ran through her list as she hurried home. Passport. Bag. Cash. Jaxon's gun. She had a feeling that would come in handy.

She reached her apartment and ran inside looking over everything as she went. She crossed her bedroom and entered her closet. She grabbed her bad quickly from under a pile of clothes and returned to her bedroom. She tossed it on the bed before opening the drawer next to it, grabbing her passport under her new name, Stacy, and the gun she took from Nicolai. She shoved them all into her bag and stood up.

Looking around one last time she grabbed her bag and left the room. As she reached the living room, something out of place caught her eye. A bouquet of roses stood on the table before her. Red, long stem roses.

She felt like she had been punched in the gut as dread pooled in her stomach. Her senses went on high alert. The air was still, but she still felt a chill. No sound reached her ears. A scent drifted towards her and his cologne assaulted her nose, bringing tears to her eyes.

She knew he was behind her before she ever turned. She wanted to run, she was only steps to the door, but she had made that mistake before. She knew the only way to end this and have any chance of survival was to face him head on. She had trained for this, but it would never be enough.

Slowly, she turned to face him. He stood there looking like nothing was out of the ordinary, like he was just there for a friendly visit. He lazily leaned against the door frame, looking over her with an easy smile. She was reminded how easily he had fooled her, how he had fooled everyone. He was charming, likeable, handsome, an upstanding member of society. He didn't look like the scum he really was.

"Lawrence," Fiona finally greeted, her hatred for him evident in the way she spat his name.

"Looking good, Fiona, looking real good. Have you been working out? For me, I hope," he chuckled. "No kiss for your husband?"

"Ex-husband," she reminded, fighting the urge to shutter under his lecherous gaze.

"I brought you roses," he redirected, pointing to the table now behind her.

"You shouldn't have," she replied seriously.

"Oh, don't be that way, Fiona. I'm your husband. It's my job to bring you nice things." He pushed away from the door and began stalking towards her.

"Ex-husband," she reiterated, standing her ground.

"About that," he sneered, his face contorting into the evil hidden within. "It's time we talked."

***

The yelling began as they scoured the mansion, going from room to room looking for anyone they might have missed. Officers in riot gear called out to one another, clearing each space as they traveled deeper into the Mafia's main base of operations. Guns, money, and drugs decorated nearly every room they passed, but they seemed devoid of another living creature.

As the last room was cleared, everyone gathered in the main living room once more. The rest of the Mafia family Jaxon had been infiltrating for the last four years sat around, handcuffed and relieved of any and all weapons. Once receiving the all clear that everyone was accounted for, Jaxon removed his face mask. He was glad it was over.

"I guess you were right," he smirked at the Don who was staring at him.

"I'm always right," the prisoner responded.

"Haier," Bertotti called out as he walked over to him. He clapped his hand on his shoulder in greeting. "Good job."

"Thanks boss," Jaxon replied, nodding his appreciation.

"It was good to have you on the project," Bertotti stated, looking around at the haul. "Just a few more days and you'll be free to move on from this place."

Jaxon grunted his response. Bertotti knew he had been itching to get out of Italy and on to the next project. He rarely stayed in once place for long, but things had changed. He had to find a way to keep Fiona.

"Actually," Jaxon began, clearing his throat. "I may need some time off."

"Really?" Bertotti gasped. "In all the years, I've never seen you ask for time off. What's up?"

"Maybe it's just time," Jaxon hedged.

"Maybe he finally found him a lady friend," one of the other officers chimed in, garnering a laugh out of several others.

"Oh come on, Jaxon taking time off for some broad? That's a stretch!" Bertotti balked.

"She would have to be pretty special," another voice added. This time, however, all laughter stopped and everyone turned towards the sound. The Don sat there with a Cheshire cat grin.

"Shut up, scum bag!" one of the other officers spat. "What would you know?"

"Oh...more than you think," he replied. "I told her I would figure her out, that I would learn her secrets, and I have."

Jaxon's blood ran cold at the crime boss' words. What had he found out? What had he done? The adrenaline rush of a good bust waivered as alarm creeped in. He needed to know how much he knew, but he couldn't ask him in front of all these people. Her life could literally hang in the balance.

"Who is he talking about, Haier?" Bertotti questioned. "Oh shit, there really is a girl, isn't there?"

"Bertotti, I gotta go. I want him in a box, on ice. No one speaks to him before I do. Can you do that?" Jaxon requested, pulling his phone out of his pocket.

"I'll see what I can do," Bertotti replied. "Where are you going?"

"I have to check on something," Jaxon called over his shoulder.

"Or someone," the Don smirked. "You're already too late, you know. She should have a very enthusiastic visitor very soon."

Jaxon stopped mid stride, his hands immediately balled into fists. He turned and marched over to the shackled crime lord and got directly in his face.

"What did you do?" he demanded.

"I got a call for a favor, one I was willing to grant," the other man answered.

Jaxon snatched him up by the front of his shirt, holding him at eye level. "I swear, if anything happens to her..."

"Haier!" Bertotti warned. "What's going on?!"

"Tick tock officer. Do you explain yourself and waste precious time? Or do you go rogue and try to find her yourself? And will it matter in the end or will you still be too late either way?" The man's laughter rang through Jaxon and his words incited his rage.

"I'll deal with you later," Jaxon growled, shoving him back to his seat. "Nothing sir. Gotta run. Again, in a box on ice. Got it?" he reminded as he jogged away.

"I don't answer to you, Haier!" Bertotti shouted down the hall, bewildered by Jaxon's change in demeanor.

"I know!"

Jaxon hurried to his car, ice water running through his veins. Jamming the key in the ignition, the car roared to life. He was about to put the car in gear when his cell dinged with a voicemail notification. Ignoring it, he put the car in reverse but stopped before he pulled out. A thought hit him. Was it Fiona?

He snatched his phone out of his pocket and felt his breath leave his lungs forcefully. His hand hovered over the name and the world around him crawled to a stop. Mackenzie. Fiona. It had been her. He slowly put the car back in park.

He hadn't heard her voice in four tortuous days. They had been forced into underground bunkers to plan the raid, no one in or out to minimize leaks. No calls. No texts. No phones at all. Nothing. It had been hell. He knew he was running out of time to find a way to clear her name and that wasn't helping.

As much as he wanted to hear her voice, though, a message didn't bode well. He remembered the Don's words echoing in his mind. She would have a visitor soon. It couldn't be Lawrence, could it? He was still in prison in the states, right? But who else could it be? Was there someone else she had crossed paths within her years of running that she didn't tell him?

He forced himself to hit the button. Just the sound of her voice soothed his battered soul. A smile sprang to his face as she said his name, but it was short lived. As she spoke, pain washed over him. He was out of time. She was running and he would never find her again. Even if she had been calling him for help, he had been unreachable, unable to save her...again.

He looked at the time. Twenty minutes. She had called twenty minutes prior and his phone had just now connected to service as the mansion had a scrambler. He slammed his hand into the dashboard in frustration. He wasn't far from her house. Maybe, just maybe, she was still there. He prayed she hadn't gotten far. He had to find her in time. He couldn't let her face that monster alone again.

He dialed her number as he drove, praying she would answer. No such luck. The line just rang and rang without even a voicemail to pick up. He found it odd that it was ringing at all if she had already left. He thought that would be the first thing she would dump, removing the battery to ensure it couldn't be turned on remotely. It made it too easy to track her.

Hoping that was a good sign that she was still nearby, he stayed his course. He wove in and out of traffic, honking his horn and yelling at people who couldn't hear him through their own rolled up windows. Desperation had him driving recklessly, relying on his days of racing in high school.

Thinking back to those times, he grit his teeth and gripped the steering wheel until his knuckles were white. Lawrence had been around in those days as well, and still just as slimy. They had faced off on the track more times than he could count. Lawrence had always been a smooth talker, and always after Fiona. Jaxon had told her as much one night, but she never believed him. She had always been pretty oblivious to guys flirting with her.

One night in particular, Jaxon had been racing his motorcycle and had smoked Lawrence, leaving him in the dust. The crowd had cheered, Lawrence had graciously admitted defeat, and that was that. Or so Jaxon had thought. On his way home from the track, Lawrence had come out of no where and tossed something into the front wheel of Jaxon's bike, causing it to lock up and throwing him over the handlebars at 40 miles an hour.

Jaxon landed on a narrow tree stump, piercing his side. Lawrence had stopped long enough to sneer at him, sending his regards to Fiona. Jaxon had never told her or anyone else the truth. He didn't want to give him the satisfaction of putting his name on Fiona's lips. That, and he knew what her reaction would have been. She would have gone directly to his house and kicked his ass and the ass hat would have pressed charges.

In hindsight, he should have told her. Maybe if he had, she wouldn't have gone to him to get back at Jaxon. Maybe, by telling her, he could have saved her. Or not. She always was a stubborn one when her mind was made up. Nothing and no one could stop her when she decided something. It was something he had always loved about her, but damn it could be exhausting.

There was no parking when he reached her apartment so he just stopped in the middle of the street. He jumped out and ran to her door, a variety of expletives called after him as the people trying to maneuver around his car shouted out their frustrations. When he reached her door, he pounded on it hard, understanding washing over him as it swung open under his touch. The thud of it hitting the wall echoed throughout, matching the pounding in his chest.

"Mac?!" he called out, unsure of who could hear him and not wanting to give her away. "Are you here?"

He stepped further into the room and stopped cold. The place was trashed. The couch had slash marks through it, stuffing spilling out onto the floor. The table was smashed to pieces, roses ground into the carpet around the debris. Sheetrock dust floated along the air, presumably from the several holes where a fist or other body part had slammed into it.

As he continued through the apartment, each room he came to held the same story. This wasn't her covering her tracks. There were shoe prints that were too large to be hers. He had been there, lying in wait for her to return, to ambush her. The ass hat had brought her roses.

"Fucking roses," he muttered as he thought.

Lawrence was even more of a tool if he thought that roses were going to atone for his sins. But one thing was certain. He may have ambushed her, but she gave as good as she got. She had been better prepared this time. He could vaguely follow the fight by their footsteps, roses and dirt ground into the carpet. The smudges along the wall and debris outlining where someone would have been also told of the fight. She had stood her ground and fought him with everything she had if the state of her apartment was any indication.

But in the end, it hadn't been enough. She wasn't dead, and neither was he, Jaxon surmised by the lack of a body or enough blood to matter. That only left one option. He had her. What did he want with her? Where would he take her? Could he get to her in time?

He cursed loudly in the empty apartment. He had nothing to go by, no loud map with shiny blinking arrows pointing him in the right direction. Lawrence hadn't been in the area long, and they had raided all of the Mafia houses, so what did that leave? How could he have found something in such a short amount of time?

Jaxon kicked himself for not thinking of it sooner. Her cell phone. Was it possible that she still had it on her? Had Lawrence found it and tossed it? Did he know Jaxon was in the area and *wanted* him to follow them? Was this a trap?

It didn't matter to Jaxon if it was a trap or not, he had to go anyway. He couldn't leave her in that man's hands, no matter the cost. He picked up his phone and opened the tracking app he had used previously to find her. He waited several long seconds before an error message came back to him. The app was spotty at best and unable to ping her signal. Cursing, he dialed his boss.

"I need a favor, and I don't have time to explain," Jaxon stated without preamble.

"Is this about the girl you and the Don were talking about?" Bertotti asked. The silence on the line was all the answer he needed. "Hit me."

"I need a phone trace, and I need it yesterday. Can you do that?"

"Sure thing."

Jaxon rattled off her number, thanking him for helping before disconnecting the line.

He paced around the small home, looking for any other clue as to where he could have taken her, where he could have been hiding. His heart formed a lump in his throat, choking him more and more the longer he waited for a response from Bertotti.

He had to reach her in time.

Relief flooded him when his phone dinged. An address lit up his screen and he sucked in a huge gulp of air. He plugged it into his GPS on his phone before running to his car, which had caused quite the backup by that point. He jumped inside the still running vehicle and forced his way into traffic.

"Hang on Fi," he said in the empty space. "I'm coming for you."

Chapter 13

Fiona glared daggers across the dimly lit cabin. Ropes bit into her wrists as she strained against them. They were tied behind her, around the back of the most uncomfortable wooden chair she had ever had the displeasure of sitting in. Her shoulders burned from the tension of her current position and she felt exposed to Lawrence's wandering eyes, wherever he was. She fought to focus through the haze of whatever he had used to drug her. She needed to be as alert as possible when he returned.

The cabin was devoid of most furniture and almost all light. The air was stale. No currents moved around the dust filled air, leaving it all feeling old and suffocating. The furniture that was still there was broken down, some in pieces. The windows were so covered in grime and newspapers that she couldn't make out anything through them to try to see where she was or what time of day it was.

Looking towards the door, she found her bag laying next to it. Hope bloomed inside of her. If he was dumb enough to bring it along, maybe he hadn't looked inside. Maybe the gun was still in there. Propelled by that thought, she began working the ropes on her wrists. Thankfully, she had prepared for such a situation. She just had to keep her wits about her and not panic.

Footsteps echoed through the small room, alerting her to his impending presence. Her heart rate jumped, as she realized she was running out of time. If she could keep him talking, she still had a chance. She doubted he would just walk in and kill her as he had obviously brought her here for a reason. He would have just finished her off in her apartment otherwise.

"Oh darling," his voice called out to her with a sing-song lilt.

Just the sound of his voice turned her stomach.

"Oh good, you're awake!" he exclaimed as he entered the room. "I was afraid I had given you too much and you'd be asleep all day."

"Untie me, Lawrence," Fiona demanded in a low voice.

"All in due time, my love," he stated, grabbing a half-broken chair and bringing it to sit in front of her. He straddled it as he stared at her.

"You don't know what love is," she spat, glaring at him.

"Oh, don't be that way. Didn't I take care of you? Love you? Treat you right?"

"Oh sure, right up to the point that you stabbed me in the back...literally," she reminded, wriggling her wrists slowly.

"That wasn't my fault and you know it," he screeched, losing the easy-going attitude. "You made me! If you hadn't shown up without calling, we would still be happily together in our house!"

Fiona kept her mouth shut. She knew the truth. She had never been happy with him and Jaxon had come back for her. Beyond that, he would have eventually shown his hand, one way or another. No. They would have ended no matter what.

Lawrence took a deep, relaxing breath. The mask slid back in place as charm replaced the crazy look in his eyes. The cracks in his façade were getting larger and Fiona knew it wouldn't take much to push him over the edge for good. She had to tread lightly. He was unstable at best and full-blown psychotic at worst.

She waited patiently to see what his next move was, slowly trying to work her hands free. One wrist was finally getting loose and that was all she needed to get away. One hand free. Apparently, he was still as cocky as ever, expecting her to still be the victim. Not this time.

"So, how have you been Fiona?" he asked sweetly. "You don't write, you don't call..."

"Didn't you get the letter I sent? Through my attorney?" she punctuated the last word with a growl.

"Oh, pish posh," he said waving his hand in the air. "I don't count that one. No piece of paper can ever undo our love. Besides, I know you were forced into it, forced into all of it."

She bit the inside of her mouth to keep from responding. She wanted to scream that she had never loved him, but she had to bide her time. She wasn't yet ready to strike.

"But you look good!" he admired, not bothered by her lack of response. "Been working out? It's good to see you've been keeping yourself busy...seeing the world...not just sitting at home waiting for me."

He had snapped. Somewhere along the line, either before they met or after, he had lost his mind. Had he always been this broken? This delusional? Had she been too blinded by her own bitterness to see the change or had it always been there?

"Well, I'm glad you got all that out of your system," he continued. "We can go home now. Settle back down. I hear our old house is on the market after an unfortunate event with the previous owners. We can move back in and forget the last eight ish years ever happened."

"I'm not going anywhere with you," she replied, unable to keep quiet as her stomach rolled with the thought of their house. She hadn't been back inside since the day she was taken out by stretcher.

Lawrence laughed sarcastically, looking around the room before turning back to her. "News flash, darling, you already have."

"Across town is one thing. Across an ocean is something completely different," she reminded him.

"Well, that's why we're here. We need to talk things through. To get on the same page."

"The only page I'm getting on, is away from you. I divorced you for a reason. I'm not going back with you," she stated cautiously.

"You think you can go running back to Jaxon? Oh wait, you would have to look through the cemeteries to do that. I wonder if he was ever given a head stone," he smirked.

Fiona stopped herself from responding immediately. If he didn't know Jaxon was alive, she wasn't going to be the one to tell him. She did, however, want to know why he believed that. "What do you mean?"

"You really think it was a coincidence that he just disappeared?" he asked incredulously. "You're dumber than I thought!"

She bristled under his assessment of her, but fought her impulse to lash out. "What did you do?" she asked instead.

"It was no secret I wanted you, but you were too hung up on that looser." His eyes took on a far away look as he told his story.

Dread filled Fiona's entire being. Jaxon had tried to warn her, but she had dismissed it. How much truth had there been?

"I really thought after that motorcycle accident that would be the end of him."

Chills ran down her spine. That wreck, the one that left the scar on his side, it had almost killed him. The images of his body, broken and drained of color, lying on a hospital bed hooked up to machines sprang to mind. She was the reason he was alive. She hadn't left his side and when he was discharged, she had taken him to her house and nursed him back to health. His father would have let him die.

She always thought there was more to the story. He was never reckless on his bike. She had asked him a million times, but he had held firm. The shock of being right all along stunned her speechless.

"I underestimated your stubbornness," he chuckled. "Not the next time though."

"What next time?" she whispered, her voice failing her.

"I can't believe his dad hated him that much...maybe he just loved money more? I don't know. Either way, money talks and that guy listened."

Fiona held her breath. He couldn't mean what she thought, could he? Jaxon's dad had taken him away and locked him in a basement. Had he done that for money? Was Jaxon supposed to be dead? Where would he have gotten that kind of cash? And how much?

"You killed him?" It was a question, an accusation. It was a request to hear more, knowing that Jaxon was safely still alive.

"Oh, I didn't. His own father did!" Lawrence replied cheerfully. "And you came running to me just like I knew you would. You know a real alpha male when you see one."

Fiona's stomach turned sour and she felt the queasiness growing inside her, threatening to escape the only way it knew how. She had truly married a monster. Her anger at Jaxon had been totally misplaced, she had recently learned, but never knew that there had still been more. She had been manipulated and played right into his hand.

"You asshole!" she shouted, unable to contain the anger building within her.

Lights danced before her eyes as his hand came out of nowhere, connecting with her cheekbone and sending her head flying to the side. Her ears rang from the unexpected contact and she had to fight to focus on anything, but her plan had worked. The force of the blow had twisted her enough to pull her loose wrist the rest of the way through the rope.

Her hands were free, but she still waited. She rubbed her wrists while her head fought through the haze of pain. She needed to be as clear headed as possible when she made her move. She might only have one shot.

"I'm not an asshole!" he spewed. "I'm driven! I know what I want and I take it! I wanted you and he was in my way, so I did what had to be done!"

He took deep calming breaths, regaining the look of control as he righted his now prone chair and sat back down. He ran his hand through his hair and smiled at her.

"I'm only telling you all of this so you know not to go looking for him. It's a waste of time. This way, you know he's gone for good, and you and I can be happy again."

Fiona shook her head to clear the last of the fog. She had to move soon. He was getting more and more unstable by the minute. It wouldn't take long for him to have a full mental break and snap her neck. No. She had to take her chance.

"I don't care if you were the last person on Earth, we could never be happy!" she ground through her teeth.

Anger flared through him as he jumped to his feet and charged at her. She was ready for him this time and she kicked out, smashing her foot squarely into his knee cap. He dropped instantly with a howl, pain lacing through him. Not stopping, Fiona brought her chair over her head as she stood, slamming it down on his head and neck, knocking him the rest of the way to the ground.

Leaping over his crumbled heap, she sprinted across the room to her bag. She ripped it open as she dropped to the floor, throwing things aside as she searched for the one thing to end this once and for all.

His laughter behind her froze her in place. It was sardonic, maniacal. He clapped slowly as he sat up to stare at her, a shit eating grin on his face.

"Good show!" he complimented, pulling himself to his feet. "Looking for this?"

Fiona cursed under her breath, tossing the bag to the side and standing up.

"This is a beaut!" he commented appreciatively. "Too bad it has to go this way. We could have ruled the world together."

Fiona's breath hitched as she stared down the barrel of the pistol she had taken from Jaxon. She knew she had pushed too far to try to back track now. Lawrence had broken and this was it. He was prepared to kill her now and there was no turning back.

"Say hi to Jaxon for me! I guess you two will be together after all." His voice was dripping with disdain as he cocked the pistol.

She sprang into motion, fear and instinct propelling her forward. A shot rang out as she dodged to the side.

"I will," she shouted, tackling Lawrence to the ground.

***

Jaxon slammed the car in park and leaped from it, running faster than he ever thought possible towards the abandoned cabin at the base of Mt. Etna. Another car sat out front and he knew it had to be Lawrence's. This is where the GPS had led him. Fiona had to be inside.

A gun shot rang out, stopping his heart and stealing his breath. No other sound reached him as he waited, afraid to move. Two more shots rang out and the spell holding him in place was broken. He was on the front porch in a flash and kicked the door open.

The sight before him halted his momentum and pierced his soul. Blood ran across the dull hardwood floors and a sticky metallic smell mingled with the scent of gun powder, filling the air. Dead eyes stared back at him, a bullet hole between them.

"Fi?" Jaxon called out soothingly.

Her back was towards him. His words seemed to have no effect on her so he slowly made his way over to her. He carefully placed his hands on her shoulders to announce his presence. She never flinched. Her eyes were locked on the lifeless body before her. Lawrence was dead.

"Fi?" he tried again.

"It was him or me," she said shakily.

"I know," he reassured her. "It's over now."

Jaxon knew the look on her face, he had seen it many times over the years on many different people. Shock was taking over. He slowly slid his hands down her arms towards the gun. "Just let me have this," he said calmly.

As if realizing she was still holding it for the first time, she immediately released it. It dropped safely into his hand as she turned into his chest. He exhaled slowly as he wrapped his arms around her. The sight of her holding a smoking gun over a dead body was one he would have a hard time forgetting.

He kissed the top of her head as he held her tight. He stared at Lawrence, wishing he had been the one to pull the trigger, but knowing it needed to be her. This was her nightmare. She needed to be the one to end it.

"It was him all along," she muttered through her tears. "It was all his fault! All these years! I couldn't let him hurt you! Not again!"

"What?" Jaxon couldn't follow her broken thoughts. What did she mean, all his fault? He thought it had been obvious that Lawrence had been behind her pain all along. Was there more he didn't know? Just as he opened his mouth to ask more, the sound of police sirens reached his ears.

"Fi, listen to me. The police will be there in a minute. Don't say a word. Not a single word. You hear me?" he coached.

She nodded her response in his chest.

"I need to hear you say it," he pressed, forcing her to look at him.

"Not a word," she promised.

He kissed her hard, pulling her to him and pouring every ounce of love and strength into it. He needed her to stay strong in the coming days. He needed to feel her against him as well.

Together, they made their way outside to the porch. He led her to sit on the stairs and he placed the gun on the hood of the car before joining her. He wrapped a reassuring arm around her while they waited, each trying to prepare for the days ahead.

"I love you, Fi," he reminded her.

"I love you, too. I always have."

"Remember, not a word. Let me handle it. I'll get you out as soon as I can," he promised. "I'll take care of everything."

Fiona was frozen inside. Lawrence was dead and she had killed him. He couldn't get her anymore. She was free of him, yet still trapped. She would never fully be free. Too much had happened.

The fight flashed before her eyes as she leaned against Jaxon. She had tackled him to the floor, knocking the gun out of his hand. Sitting up, she slammed her fists into his face, over and over before leaping off of him and scrambling for the gun. His hand had wrapped around her ankle as her fingers reached the cold steel, flinging it the other way as he pulled hard.

Her foot kicked him solidly in the face, knocking him away before she jumped to her feet and raced for the gun. As her fingers wrapped around the grip, she turned and fired. Twice. He dropped like lead, blood pooling around him.

She had wanted to do more. She wanted to tear him limb from limb with her bare hands, to make him suffer like she had suffered. But in the end, she had just wanted it over. He wasn't worth losing what was left of her soul.

Blue and red lights flashed before her eyes. Jaxon kissed her one last time, his touch lingering on her battered heart. She followed his instructions, but more out of shock than self-preservation.

Her mind was numb. The world around her was nothing but a haze. She had been ripped away from Jaxon, her only anchor through the storm raging inside her, as his promises to come for her followed her into the police car. She watched him argue with someone through the window as they drove her away, his muffled shouts drowned out by the sound of the road.

Then there was processing, questioning, being thrown into a cell with four other people. Through it all, she never opened her mouth, never uttered a word. She heard someone call it shock and call for a doctor, but she didn't care.

"Miss? Miss!"

She blinked at the sound of someone speaking to her. She fought to focus her eyes on their face and her ears to listen.

"You're free to go," the man before her repeated. "Are you okay? Did you hear me? Someone pretty high up must have your back."

Fiona blinked away the confusion and followed the person speaking to her. She wondered what Jaxon had had to do to save her, to get her out. She knew the only way to save herself from this mess was to tell them everything, but it would be admitting who she was. She hated to think what he had to give up for her and hugged her recently returned bag to her chest.

Blinking against the afternoon as she stepped out of the police station, she wondered how long she had been in there. Everything had been a blur and days had bled together. She knew Jaxon would want to see her, but she also knew how much harder that would be. There was only one thing left for her to do now.

She boarded a bus going to the coast and sat back. She barely noticed the city she had learned to love as she passed through it. Her heart broke as she traveled, knowing what was coming next. Images of Jaxon ran through her head; a past they never got to complete and a future that could never be. A love that could never exist. She was thankful for the stolen time they had together, but she knew it couldn't continue. The memories would have to be enough.

As she reached the coast, she made her way to the nearest ferry. Tears streamed silently down her face as her feet slowly climbed the plank. She watched as the shore moved further and further away, putting distance between her and her one true love.

"Good-bye, Jax," she muttered to the open air. "I love you."

Chapter 14

2 years later

Wind blew through the trees, rustling the leaves and playing in the grass. Flowers adorned the headstone of a lonely grave in the middle of the graveyard at the heart of Atlanta, Georgia. The sun warmed the air and the birds sang overhead.

Elenore ran her hand lovingly along the strong granite. Her brown eyes caressed the words etched within as her blond hair drifted on the breeze. She sighed, a sound of both contentment and sadness. 10 years. 10 years had come and gone with rarely anyone any wiser.

She read the name. Fiona Lancaster. An orphan. Divorced. Alone. No one, save her best friend, to care she was gone. Destined to travel the afterlife on her own.

"Hey, Fi," Elenore began as she sat in the soft grass. "It's been a while. Too long. Or not long enough."

She took a deep steadying breath, trying to find the right words.

"I've done things you never got to. I traveled to the places you only dreamed of. France. Morocco. Italy. England. Costa Rica. Germany. Greece. Everywhere in between. I've met amazing people and the scum of the earth.

"I've trained. I've danced. I've been homeless on a beach and I've lived in a penthouse. I've been whoever I wanted to be without expectation. I've become a master of blending in, of running, of hiding. I've traveled the world without ever leaving a mark. Well...except one.

"Italy." The name was said with a swirl of emotion. She took a moment to look skyward, taking deep breaths.

"Your past came back to haunt us. Both paths your life could have taken converged in that tiny tourist town. Your one true love...and the man who tried to kill you both.

"As far as that ass hat goes...he's dead. I made sure of that. He didn't leave me much of a choice. I know that I promised you I would, and I trained for it almost daily, but it was still traumatizing. It took over a year and several countries to get the image of him dead on the floor out of my head. And the things he said...the things he confessed to...all the pain he caused...well...that may never leave.

"Now Jaxon...he's much harder to forget, not that I would ever want to. His love is what every woman should have every day of her life. He was a light in the darkness, but was stolen away once more."

Anger bubbled inside of her. "Damn it, Fiona!" she shouted. "You never should have given up! You should have known he would never leave you! Damn you and your stupid pride!"

Tears ran down her face, but she made no attempt to stop them. "Then I ran. Now neither of us can have his love, but at least I have the memories. I'll always remember Italy. My heart will always stay there, with him. I can still feel his lips pressed against mine, his arms wrapped around my body holding me tight. My head against his chest as we slept. I know now I should have waited for him, but at the time I just had to get away. Self-preservation took over, or maybe I was still in shock, and I ran...God I was so stupid!"

The sound of feet shuffling behind her alerted Elenore to a presence. She quickly cleaned the tears from her face and forced a cheeriness to her voice.

"I'm about done here," she called out.

"Take your time, gorgeous."

Elenore stilled at the deep male voice. She looked up towards the sky in shock, staring up at green eyes. "You aren't Jade," she managed to say.

Her heart ached at the sight of him as she stood to face him. She wanted to throw herself into his arms, to feel his body wrapped around hers, to beg him to forgive her and to love her like she still loved him, but she held herself back. He probably hated her for leaving and his rejection would break her already fragile heart.

"How long have you been standing there?" she asked, trying to gauge how much he had heard.

"Long enough," he hedged. "You're a hard woman to find."

Looking at her was like breathing fresh air for the first time in two long years. He couldn't stop the smile that spread across his face.

"That was...kinda the point," she reminded.

"You should have trusted me," he whispered, his smile never wavering.

"I know," she replied, dropping her eyes to her feet. "I'm sorry. I was scared. I was so used to having to be alone, not trusting anyone else that I did the one thing I knew to do. I ran."

"Fi-"

"Wait...you've never been anything but wonderful. You're a man of your word. If anyone could have saved me, it would have been you." She paused again, trying to find the words. "If it's any consolation, I tried to call once the shock wore off and I realized what I had done, but your number had been disconnected."

"Fiona-"

"Please don't hate me," she begged. "I didn't want to leave you. I-"

"Good God woman, would you shut up?" he chuckled. He took her hands into his, causing her gaze to return. "I've been trying to tell you. I did it. I fixed it all."

"What?" she couldn't believe her hears. Even after she had left him, he had kept trying.

"Technically, your death was sanctioned by wit-sec from the beginning. There is no insurance fraud issue. You're free," he told her softly.

"And Italy?"

"Once I explained everything, including the crime scene photos, your case was dismissed as self-defense. It helped that my boss heard the threats against you from the Don himself. It made it premeditated on their end and self-defense on yours."

Her mind raced. She was free. She was truly free to be herself again for the first time in over 10 years. No more running. No more hiding. No more secret identities. Free to live. Free to love...Jaxon.

"Jax...I...I don't...I don't know what to say..." she sputtered.

The smile that lit her face was more than he could take. He pulled her to him, kissing her with everything in him. She melted instantly into his arms, returning his kiss with equal desire. When they broke away, their breathing was shallow and ragged.

"Fi..."

"He tried to kill you, you know," she rushed to say. She needed him to know.

"I know," he replied. Her eyes widened in shock. "Mom finally told me. Or I finally asked, one. But it doesn't matter. That's over. He can't hurt you anymore."

"Jax-"

"Marry me," he interrupted.

"What?!" Stunned, she searched his face for any sign of sarcasm or hurtful joke.

"Marry me," he repeated.

"Jax...there is nothing on this earth that I want more, but...the woman you fell in love with all those years ago is in the ground right there," she said, pointing to the headstone.

"We both know we fell in love all over again in Italy," he told her smiling. "And I fell in love again when I saw you sitting in this cemetery. I want you...only you. I love you and I don't care what your first name is anymore, as long as your last name is Haier till the day we die."

True happiness began to bloom in her chest for the first time in over a decade. Her face hurt from the force of her smile as she threw herself into his arms. Their laughter rang through the air.

"I really thought I would have to try harder to convince you," he laughed.

"Don't you know you have always had my heart?" she chided. Slowly, she removed her wig and dropped it to the ground. "I won't be needing that anymore."

"Or the contacts," he reminded.

Soon, her emerald greens looked back at him lovingly and her red hair was free for all to see. Heat raced through him under her sultry gaze. Before he could reach for her, she was already wrapping her arms around his neck and pulling him down. Her lips found his as her fingers wove through his hair. She didn't need much encouragement for her lips to part enough for his tongue to plunge inside, seizing control. Her moan drove him mad and before he knew it, he had her lifted in the air, her legs wrapped around his waist.

"I've heard of dancing on people's graves before, but this is a whole other level," Jade joked, her voice making the other two freeze. "At least we know that grave is empty...that would be weird."

Fiona blushed as Jaxon slowly lowered her to the ground. They quickly remembered where they were but refused to let each other go.

"Wait," Fiona stated, looking at the lack of shock on Jade's face. "How did you find me?" She looked up at Jaxon.

"I may have called in a favor," he replied grinning.

"Don't worry, there was a lot of interrogating and begging involved. Some groveling, too," Jade assured her.

"And if I hadn't come back here today?" Fiona questioned.

"Then I would have found another way, combed the earth for you."

"Awww!" Jade squealed, clapping her hands.

"Why didn't you just have Jade pass me a message? It seems like that would have been easier...and faster..." Fiona asked, furrowing her eyebrows at them.

"Um...well...I..."

"You didn't think of that," Fiona laughed, hugging him tighter.

"This was way more romantic," Jade pointed out, backing Jaxon up. "Besides, you have only been talking to me again for like the last six months. Leaving me in the damn dark." Jade crossed her arms and glared at Fiona.

"Well, fair point," Fiona conceded.

"So...did you do it? Did you do the thing?"

"Yep!" Jaxon answered, a glow crossing his face.

"Where's the ring?! Let me see it!" Jade exclaimed, jumping up and down.

"Oh...I...he..." Fiona couldn't believe she hadn't thought about that.

"Oh...right. It all happened so fast that I forgot" he admitted, digging in his pocket.

"Did you at least drop to one knee?" Jade asked incredulously. At his sheepish expression, she clucked her tongue and pointed at the ground. "Do it, mister. Drop or it didn't happen."

"Oh he doesn't-"

"No, she's right. I need to do this right," Jaxon insisted.

Fiona held her breath as he knelt before her, taking her hand in his. She vaguely noticed Jade take her phone out and start snapping the first pictures and video of her in a decade but she was more focused on the incredibly handsome man before her.

"Fiona, I love you. I have always loved you. It has only ever been you. Not even the clinically insane or geography could keep us apart. Hell, not even death can keep us apart apparently," he laughed. "Marry me. Stop running...come home, not just to Atlanta, but to me."

He opened the ring box in front of her as his hands began to shake. Her eyes lit up at the sparkle inside and she dropped to her knees in front of him.

"You already know my answer," she joked through the happy tears. "Yes...a thousand times, yes!"

"YES! The bestie is coming home!" Jade yelled.

"You know she's going to be at our house, right? Like...a lot," Fiona giggled.

"That's fine by me," Jaxon promised. "As long as I get to go to bed with you every night and wake up beside you every day, I don't care how often your best friend is there. At our...home."

"Home. I like the sound of that."

Peace settled over her as the past melted away and she started the life she should have had all along, filled with incredible friends and a love that transcended time and space. She smiled at Jade and Jaxon as she stood up, pulling her new fiancé with her.

"Let's go home."

The End

Piper is the name Mrs. Bedwell has hidden behind since middle school, giving her a chance to be bold and fearless instead of nervous and awkward. When she isn't lost in a fantasy world or creating new stories, Piper spends her time living in the southern United States with her family: her ever supporting husband, two beautiful daughters, and a fluffle of bunnies. During her tenure as a writer, Piper has created dozens of stories with no intention of ever sharing them with the world. In 2019, she gained a little courage and received a big push. The rest is history.

The beautiful cover was created by the talented Chelsea Boone-Belcher at Boone Studios.

Printed in the USA
CPSIA information can be obtained
at www.ICGtesting.com
JSHW020805240624
65279JS00001B/1